DARK STONES

[Handwritten dedication in Portuguese, illegible in parts:]

Para o Sr. Professor
Bob Wayler, com
admirações, grato
por tudo, principal-
mente por este diá-
logo que acabamos
de manter.

New-Bedford, 16-5-88

[signature]

Dias de Melo

DARK STONES

Translated from the Portuguese by

Gregory McNab

GÁVEA-BROWN
Providence, Rhode Island

Original Title
  Pedras Negras

First Portuguese Edition
  Lisbon, 1964

Design
  Ted Ramos

Cover
  Rogério Silva/Ted Ramos

Published and distributed by
  Gávea-Brown Publications
  Center for Portuguese & Brazilian Studies
  Brown University
  Providence, R.I. 02912

Translation copyright © 1988 by Gregory McNab, Jr.

Library of Congress Catalogue Number: 83-080781

ISBN: 0-943722-05-5

"The only universal ... is what is typically local."

Gregorio Marañón

"Do not leave your own milieu in search of originality. The sun shining over your land is the same sun which lights the whole world."

João de Araújo Correia

Acknowledgement

This edition was made possible by the support of a group of *picarotos* from California.

To the memory

of my ancestors and of all those who are walled in on the Island or scattered throughout the world which lies over the horizon—they were born, they lived and they died loving always the Dark Stones of Pico.

Although the setting is a particular village on the Island of Pico in the Azores, the happenings and the people who struggle to live in the pages of this book should not be identified with events and individuals from real life.

D.M.

TABLE OF CONTENTS

PART ONE

    The Island Casts the People Out 15
    The Great Journey 31

PART TWO

    Return 73
    On the Island Forever 101

PART THREE

    And That Night There Were No Stars in the Sky 139

PART ONE

THE ISLAND CASTS THE PEOPLE OUT

(the year of the famine)

Back then, during the long evenings of Winter, in the old house, poor, cramped and with holes in the floor—his Grandfather talked about the Year of the Famine.

The neighbors arrived after supper, in the dark of night, the women wrapped up in their heavy woolen shawls, the men with their caps pulled down to their ears, and they called out:

"Good evening!"

A wave of cold came in through the half-open door, and the people inside answered:

"Good evening to you! Come in! Come in and sit down!"

By the open hearth, on the kitchen floor, the women crossed their legs under their long skirts, while the men stretched theirs out and rubbed their feet together, having slipped them out of their shoes.

In the rush basket which was hanging from the old black cedar beam burned the flame of the rusty lamp. In the hearth the embers of beech coals crackled. And a tepid, sweet warmth slipped in through damp clothing to chilled bodies.

Adolescent boys and girls danced and sang to the sounds of the guitar, which Francisco Marroco's father played better than anyone else—and the evening's festivities got livelier as the night wore on.

The women spun, carded, made socks and patched. The men talked, in slow voices, cigarettes in the corners of their mouths, in need of shaves. The children went to and fro, in a never-ending game, until tired at last, they snuggled into the warmth of their mothers' laps. Then they looked at the serious faces of the women, they heard the strumming of the guitar, the songs of the adolescents, the conversations of the men...

Francisco Marroco was very little, but he remembers...

The men talked. For long intervals, they talked exhaustively about earthquakes; much more exhaustively and for much longer intervals, they talked about the perhaps legendary fire, which long ago must have burst from the dark stones of the Island. And painfully, very painfully, there was no night when they did not talk about the difficulties and misfortunes they themselves had lived: about the constant and uncertain struggles with the land, about the disasters at sea, about such and such year of drought, about such and such year of cyclones...

And his Grandfather, with his shaky voice, his white hair, his sad eyes, began again:

"When I was a boy, there was the Year of the Famine..."

(The guitar playing, the voices singing, the men talking, could no longer be heard. And the women stopped spinning, stopped carding and patching.)

...A year before—as his Grandfather told it—on one of the last days of August, a cyclone had come. The people ran to the church, knelt in front of the statues of the saints and the crown of the Divine Holy Ghost. The sea, however, kept pounding against the rocks of the Island, rushed inland, swallowed up vineyards and grain fields. The wind swept the Island from end to end, knocked over walls, tore off roofs, uprooted trees, corn and sweet potatoes. It left the fields flattened, worse off than if fire had laid waste to them. Cut off from heaven and the World, the islanders prepared for the difficult recovery, trusting in the fish of the sea, in the animals saved from the storm, in the corn left in their houses.

"You all know how it is," his Grandfather would say. "If there's a bad year, you wait until a better one comes along. That time..."

The new year came with a Winter able to deal out anything—wind, hail, and almost no rain. The Autumn sprouted and turned out badly, and the men watched the threatening clouds unhappily.

Even so, April brought with it the appearance of Spring. A tremor of new life was flowing in everybody's veins. The weather was getting better, the rain was falling, the Sun was getting brighter. The farmers cleared the fields, spread manure, worked the land, scattered seed on the earth. The corn grew nicely, and no one remembered the Winter which began so badly nor the winds of some months back. They were all content, sure that that year would be one of plenty, and on moonlit nights, they sang and danced at the crossroads.

"Afterwards...," and the old man would take a pinch from his tobacco pouch. "The dust from our land is good! But two weeks without rain and everything begins to go bad. That time, the last rain was at the end of May. June went by without a single drop falling. The corn stalks dried up, the people were getting desperate. They turned to the Divine Holy Ghost for help—and in the late afternoon, they'd be out on the roads, in the corn fields, in processions of prayer and penitence with the crown of the Divine Holy Ghost in their hands. July came and then August arrived..."

...And the Year of the Famine had begun. Food was getting scarce. Water—the tidal pool had been clogged up by the winds—came only from the Swamp, which was dirtied with mosquitoes and cattle dung. Emaciated, their bones outlined under their thin skin, the people wandered aimlessly with burning eyes and hungry mouths—the old ones collapsing from weakness, the children pitifully wasted away in their limp little bodies. Mothers, fathers, grandparents—they looked at their children!

And in the late afternoon, the processions of prayers and penitence...

In the beginning, the animals were killed to satisfy hunger. Then, the animals began to die—and the men kept trying to overcome hunger with the remains of the animals which were dying off. Then came the epidemic: headaches, high fevers, swollen bellies, greenish diarrhea mixed with blood and pus. There were no doctors.

"The priest from Flores was the one who helped the sick. A real saint he was!" his Grandfather would say.

Yet there was no medicine which could cure that illness—and the sick died. Some days, there were five or six burials...

At night, the long black lines of wretched human ragbags kept passing each other—in their hands the crown of the Divine Holy Ghost, in their eyes the delirium of pain, in their mouths a last cry for pity.

"At the end of October, when the epidemic was dying down, there wasn't a house in these parts where death hadn't entered. Many of them were deserted, the fire in the hearth gone out. And throughout these fields—not even a stalk of corn! Not even a blade of grass alive!"

The survivors persisted in keeping breath in their bodies—and the flight began. To tell the truth, only the old, the sick and the crippled stayed. The young, the healthy and the able-bodied—they all left! For America, for Brazil, and those not as well-off or as lucky, for the other islands in the Archipelago. The Year of the Famine had gone there, too. Nevertheless, any land where the eyes of the people had not wept so many tears of grief had to be better than this one. Parents, if they themselves couldn't go, sent their children off, even the very young, anywhere, so they wouldn't have to see them die of hunger.

"It was a sorrow of the soul!" the voice of the old man almost sobbed. "Me, I stayed. My brothers, the four of them, my grandparents, my father—they'd all died. God forgot only the two of us, my mother and me. My mother, she didn't seem the same person. She'd aged more than a hundred years in those few months. And she asked me to go, too. I, well, I couldn't go without taking her with me. But she wouldn't go, said she didn't matter, said she'd been born on these dark stones and couldn't leave the land where our people were buried. My heart wouldn't let me leave her. I stayed. And I and all those of us who stayed ate dry roots, rat meat, cat meat, dog meat—to keep from starving to death."

Francisco Marroco remembers... His Grandfather, quiet, watching the flame of the lamp without seeing it; the men, their arms crossed, hands tucked into the warmth of their armpits, still, their eyelids lowered, watching the dance of the smoke from their cigarettes; the adolescents amazed, staring at the embers in the hearth; the children settling in on the laps of their mothers, who were moved and patted the heads of their children.

Francisco Marroco even thinks he sees his mother and her eyes embracing him, watery with tenderness—and fear... And his father—cigarette in the corner of his mouth, guitar clasped against his chest...

There outside, Winter was roaring on—the wind... the

sea... the rain... In the kitchen, the shadows were creeping across the blackened walls...

Fear... Everyone was afraid...

(dark stones)

"We are poor. And the poor person who doesn't scrape the bread he needs to eat from the land—he has no right to life," his father used to say.

At the age of twelve, Francisco Marroco began to go to work, to earn his daily bread under the watchful eyes of a stranger in the vineyards of Captain Grilo. There he met João Peixe-Rei, a young man who'd already been married for some time to Idalina, who was expecting their first child. The news had brought João Peixe-Rei joy and anguish, and anxiety. All he talked about was the child who would come and of his wish to give it a better life—and his companions, tired of being fathers many times over, had neither the patience nor the understanding to listen to him.

"Your child—you don't know whether it'll be a boy or a girl—will be just like anyone else's," they said. And added harshly: "Or do you think you're better than the rest of us?"

And bent towards their work, they moved off.

Francisco Marroco, taken by his words and the kind look in his face, stayed with João Peixe-Rei who, without paying any attention to the difference in their ages, opened up to Francisco and talked about his courtship of Idalina and his love for her. And then again, he talked about the child they were expecting:

"I hope he never has to know what it's like to want a piece of bread to eat, some rags to wear and not have them and no money to buy them. Even so, we get by. But if we're hit by droughts and winds? And there's nothing harder than to have to see a child suffer! Well then, a child! If I only had a piece of the whaling company..."

Sponsored by Mr. Crown, a Yankee with a maritime supply firm who had established himself on Faial to do business with shipping, Captain Silveira had started up the local whaling station, shortly after landing, and for it, there came from America a longboat which went out with the help of a fishing boat. True to his ideas, which were quite surprising for the time and the place, he had decided to set the station up as a joint partnership based on shares, owned equally and mostly by those who would be the whalers. For them, and only for them, the Captain compensated their lack of capital with interest-free loans to be paid back gradually from the salaries and dividends they would receive. In the beginning, no one wanted to take the chance. It wasn't long, however, until the earnings made everyone's mouth water. With no other boats to compete against them, the men took many whales. And hardly had the whales been boiled down in the pots set up in the shadow of the edge of a big rock at the back of the pier, when two or three boats loaded down with the barrels of oil produced set out for Faial, where Mr. Crown paid cash. Then the whalers gathered together to settle accounts. Once the few expenses had been deducted, they divided up what was left—half for partners, half for whalers. And since they were both whalers and partners, they received a good-sized sum. But, with only one rowboat and one sailboat to crew...

"No! I can't go off whaling," João Peixe-Rei said resignedly. "I have to live off the land. And for those who live off the land... Well, the land's not to blame. You can't ask more of anyone who's given what he can. Look at those fields!"

They had just eaten and the two of them were resting in a cave. In front of Francisco Marroco's eyes rolled the coastal flat with its vineyards, which the dark stripes of the stone drywalls patched into the checkerboard of small corrals and long narrow walkways. Beyond them rose the hillsides, sometimes steeply, sometimes gently, as far as the edge of the upland plateau where the valleys are scattered; there the lakes rest, and the hills and mountains of the interior of the Island stand.

All those fields made up a tormented body. The most that eyes could spot on them was stone. Stone—ground and scattered in the plague of gravel in the seaside vineyards! Stone—up the slopes, piled in cairns and heavy walls which oppressed and smothered the poor corn fields! Stone—a malformed scab of a wound which never heals, rising up into massive rocks with a painful scowl! Stone—stretched in enormous slabs, in the abandonment of someone who'd thrown himself down there because he was fed up with a suffering he couldn't bear any longer! Stone—on the hills, crags and half-sunken rocks which crisscross the Island from end to end! Stone—on top of the land, underneath it, overflowing into the depths of the ocean!

"It's not the land's fault," João Peixe-Rei repeated. "Didn't your grandfather used to talk to you about the Year of the Fire?"

A few months before, Francisco Marroco had been there when his Grandfather passed away and he still carried inside himself the sore of loss and fear which he got from that first contact with the mystery and the surprise of death. He'd gotten used to seeing his always old Grandfather and never thought he'd die.

"Not my grandfather." And the way a grown-up would, he took a deep drag on what was left of his cigarette, hiding his eyes in the smoke. "I'd heard something or other, but from other people."

The break was coming to an end, and already some workers were back at their digging in the grey light of the Winter's afternoon. In the southwest, the ominous-looking clouds were winding in together. They were spreading over the sky, darkening the land and the sea. The rain fell, first in large heavy drops, then in densely packed small ones, finally in a violent downpour which was whipped by the sea wind. Again the workers ran for cover. João Peixe-Rei, inside the cave, tucked Francisco into the best corner. And he took off his sweater and wrapped the boy up in it.

"Get comfortable," he suggested. And he talked about the Year of the Fire. "Father Velho—you couldn't remember him—he used to talk about it." And in another tone of voice, "You been to Silvado's knoll, at the end of the rim, at the crater?"

Yes, Francisco Marroco had already gone to the top of Silvado's knoll and seen the crater.

João Peixe-Rei explained, "On almost all the knolls of the Island a vent opened: each knoll must have been a volcano and each crater an opening!"

At the time when men first came to the Island, they found it peppered with stone, which had been spit out by the volcanoes: colossal stones, heaped on top of each other, like those you can see scattered over the boulders and crags of the coast; small stones, gravel, fields and fields of gravel. At first sight, the men must have felt small, crushed, terrified—and perhaps with their arms hanging at their sides and their heads down, they let themselves fall into the conformity brought about by tears. They found themselves alone, for the World had forgotten them.

"Even today," João Peixe-Rei lamented, "the rulers of the kingdom only remember the people when it's time to collect the taxes." And he continued:

"But the wretches lifted their heads up. They were men. They would give in, but it would be struggling, arms stiffened, hands clawing, struggling against the dark stones of the Island. They broke the surface, they dug, they removed, they opened passage, and the earth began to appear! Dusted in thin layers over flagstones and gravel beds, it was scattered in gullies and on slopes, easily washed away by winds and rains, packed into narrow, deep ravines, which barely left space on the surface for a dozen feet of wheat. But it was earth! Earth which would mean bread and life! Hands calloused and spirits moved by the light of new hope—they turned to the dust of the earth: they dragged it, straightened it out, smoothed it; they fixed it into narrower plots, more warmed by the sun, less at the mercy of the winds. Along gullies and slopes, they built strong dark walls which were both rubble and bulwark, and with them, they shored up the earth in the long zigzagging series of small fields which rise up there in a stairway of terraces. The leftover stone they piled up in the middle and in the corners of the gardens and enclosures. There, in the seaside uplands, there was hardly a trace of earth. They tried planting the vines for grapes among the gravel in the gaps between the slabs and between the smoothed stones. If the stohy layer became too thick, they dug holes fifteen to twenty palms deep and seven to ten wide at the mouth—and down there they planted the vine.''

And João Peixe-Rei looked at those fields:

"Today, in the Spring, people look at all that green and can't imagine what the others suffered to get it that way!"

The wind had died down. The sky hovered low over the Island, black and as heavy as lead. A soft rain was falling, but it was steady and dense. Under cover, the workers kept their gaze on the red eye and smoke of their cigarettes. João Peixe-Rei told what he'd heard from Father Velho:

"Over on this side of the Island, we were some of the ones who'd had the worst luck. We worked and we suffered, and we're still working and suffering—but what the first ones did has lasted, if not forever, at least until our days. A few earthquakes, not much more. The unlucky ones were those who settled over there, around the mountain, because they are the ones who suffered in the Year of the Fire."

...The earth began to shake, the fire burst out, and the light from the flames and the rumblings from the land—they filled the Island, the sea, they spread to all the islands of the Archipelago. Dark ashes clouded the sky and you couldn't tell day from night. The people abandoned their houses, ran to the churches, took shelter under the Crown of the Divine Holy Ghost and fled, dragging with them the old people, the children, the sick, the crippled. The wave of humanity surged aimlessly along the pockmarked roads, through the passages along the ground, in the open, deep cracks. And the wretched went from village to village, prostrated themselves on the stone floors of the churches, hoarsely begged heaven's mercy—and again they moved on and again they fled. The earth contined to shake and rumble, the flames continued to rise above the top of the mountain, the ashes contined to cloud the sky, blinding the light of day, falling on the Island. Dozens of mouths vomited up fire—on the flanks of the mountains, down here, on the roads, on the fields, into the sea, for something around half a league along the coast. And streams of lava rose from the sea against the suffering body of the Island. From Silveira over there in the south, from Prainha de Cima up north, the Island was a bonfire. People believed the end of the world had come. And when land and sea stopped vomiting fire, and stone, and lava, the Island in those places was a huge cemetery—a terrible common grave of smoking stone and boulders, which had swallowed houses, churches, lands!

"Did many die?" Francisco Marroco wanted to know.

As far as João Peixe-Rei was concerned, that's how Father Velho had told it. It had been a miracle: only two from São João died—a moorish slave who was filling the fountain of a house with water, and a man who'd been foolish enough to get too close to the fires.

And when the cataclysm had passed, those who could set out for the World, especially for Brazil. Those who stayed struggled against hunger, against illness, against death. They fell, but not without a fight. And those who still felt traces of strength in their arms remained standing, stubbornly standing, hanging on to life. The Island, for them, went back to being what it had been for the first settlers, a mountain of stone. And like the first settlers, once more they moved the stone aside and removed the gravel in search of the lost soil. And once more, they rearranged and fixed up and set right the soil they uncovered—which would produce bread again. And they rebuilt their houses and reconstructed their churches. There were places, however, flatlands and more flatlands, wrapped forever in the stone shroud vomited up by the volcanoes, that neither the iron of the spade nor the blade of the plow ever touched again. They are the *mistérios*.

"You've never gone to any of those places in the North or the South?" João Peixe-Rei asked.

No. Francisco Marroco had never left the village.

"So, you've never seen the *mistérios*. There's one at Silveira, one at São João, one at Terra do Pão, one at Prainha, another at Bandeiras, at Santa Luzia and one at São Roque. Not even the toughest plants can set down roots in so much stone!"

The afternoon was getting on, the wind was northeast and the air had gotten chilly. The workers were getting impatient:

"This rain's never going to stop!"

João Peixe-Rei looked at the blackness of the waterlogged vines. His lips tightened on his cigarette. Nearby the monotonous sound of the sea against the rocks went on.

"The Island casts us out!" he said. "Years of drought, cyclones and the fire which never promised never to burst out again... And for a person to know he'll be raising a son in this kind of place. If I could just get away from here! The ones who go get rich. Captain Silvestre, who's out there now, and the owner of this vineyard, Captain Grilo... Have you seen Captain Grilo?''

One day Francisco Marroco, who was still a boy, had seen Captain Grilo's whaler anchored in front of the port. And he had seen the captain—tall, strong, straight, well-dressed—and passed close to him.

And João Peixe-Rei talked about Captain Grilo:

...He'd been born in the village to a poor family and when he was still a kid, he'd sneaked off and shipped out. He became a ship's captain and sailed the seas hunting whales. Whenever he unloaded his barrels full of oil in New Bedford and went back out to sea, he'd always make for Azorean waters and drop anchor here, in view of his homeland. He'd bring things for his relatives and friends, and there'd be big parties and food and drink. He'd bought some vineyards and each trip, he bought more to add to them; and in the winehouse he'd built, he felt himself reassured by the red verdelho wine aging in well decantered barrels, by the morcela, the bacon and the linguiça,which his brothers stored. Within a week, more or less, after his ship disappeared over the horizon, it was more than a sure thing that some of the young men of the village were gone.

"The last time, he took my brother," said João Peixe-Rei. "The navy's oarsmen really search and even a gunboat makes the rounds, but they always manage to get away!

"I want to tell you something. But you have to swear you'll be as quiet as the stones. Don't even tell your mother what I'm going to tell you!"

"I can keep a secret!" declared Francisco Marroco.

"When Captain Grilo comes, I'm going to ask him to take me. But keep your mouth shut, because that dirty mob of oarsmen would love to get their hooks into anyone thinking about slipping away without saying anything. And I don't have any money to grease their palms."

(it's not the earth of Pico that'll gnaw my bones)

Francisco Marroco began to feel like a man. And one night at the harvest festival...

Old, young, children—everybody was making the rounds of the vineyards and winehouses, for the picking and crushing of the grapes. The must was seeping from the pressing tubs, and at night, people danced along the roads. There was a moon—an enormous moon.

Francisco Marroco's father filled the night with his guitar strumming. His wife was sitting next to him, wrapped up in her shawl. Adolescent boys and girls were singing and couples were whirling around in the turns of the *chamarrita*.

And around in the turns of the *chamarrita* went Roque's daughter Maria in the arms of her partner. Francisco Marroco couldn't take his eyes off her: off her black hair, off her suntanned face, off her dark eyes, off her graceful body and its well-shaped bust with its dainty little breasts outlined inside her calico blouse. Trembling, his blood a fire burning his veins, Francisco Marroco got his courage up and tossed off a rhyme. She blushed and her face stiffened. But when she passed by on the promenade for the *chamarrita,* she glanced at him out of the corner of her eye, as if by chance. Francisco Marroco got bolder and when the *chamarrita* she was dancing was over, he went over and asked her to do the next one with him.

The guitar in his father's hands and the words in the throats of their singers were a symphony of emotions echoing through the vineyards, along the rocks of the coast, to be lost far off in the distance of the sea. From the sky, the moon shone down on things, souls and people—oceans of tenderness.

That's the way Francisco Marroco found his love.

Afterwards, on his way back from work, he'd leave his companions, slip cautiously along the paths and walkways to meet Maria. And they would say the same words that men and women have been saying to each other since the World became the World.

"You're the morning star that lights up my life, Maria!" And Francisco Marroco would hold the small hand of his love in his.

"My father is suspicious! If he finds out...," Maria cautioned.

"I'll speak to him," promised Francisco Marroco.

And Maria stopped showing up. Francisco Marroco, his heart sick with worry, hid from the night, flattening himself against the wall along the roadway in front of her door, looking at the window of the room where he knew she was sleeping. He came home in the early morning, with just enough time to grab his pick and begin another day of work.

And when they met again:

"My father," sobbed Maria, "I don't remember ever seeing him so angry. He beat me and locked me up at home. Today he went off to the woods. I was about to burst, I missed you so much. My mother let me come. No matter what happens, I'll be yours! Yours—or no one else's!" And she threw herself into Francisco Marroco's arms and cried, her body trembling and her head against his chest.

And for the first time, Francisco Marroco kissed that hair, those lips, those eyes which would never lie.

And he went to see old man Roque.

"You," and the old man's eyes fired up, "you, who don't even have a place where you can drop dead, marry my daughter? I'd rather see her dead! You're not good enough for her!" And with a look of scorn, "Get out, you thief!"

...And it was then that Francisco Marroco decided.

Some days later, he found João Peixe-Rei on a deserted road.

"Hey, I've been looking for you!" said his friend.

"Same here!"

And the two sat down in the shadow of a wall.

"My brother wrote. He landed in America two months ago. Captain Grilo won't be there long..."

"And you?"

"My mind's made up."

"Well..."

"My boy's growing. It won't be long before he's a man and me a worthless old has-been. I'm shipping out, if the captain'll take me."

"I want to go with you."

"You want to go with me!?"

"I do," answered Francisco Marroco firmly.

And when he'd told his love-story:

"As quickly as I can get enough money to choke that gypsy, Roque, I'll come back to marry Maria," he declared. "But just to get married and be off, I don't want any more to do with this! I've thought a lot about it! The Year of the Famine, droughts, cyclones, volcanoes' fire, earthquakes... No! It's not going to be the earth of Pico that'll gnaw my bones!"

THE GREAT JOURNEY

(over all the seas of the whole world)

In an out-of-the-way cove on the coast, huddled down between two rocks, Francisco Marroco and João Peixe-Rei looked at the ocean and remained crouched down and quiet so the navy's oarsmen wouldn't spot them. They couldn't see the whaling ship, which was riding the waters not far out, but—the captain had said so—they knew it would be that night.

The noise of the waters was not always hoarse. Sometimes it was a whistle or a whine. Francisco Marroco and João Peixe-Rei felt their hearts pound faster, hoping it wasn't the oarsmen with their carbines, their bayonets...

Francisco Marroco and João Peixe-Rei didn't even have a knife between them. They'd left home, each carrying only a pack with some rough wool garments inside.

Francisco Marroco also had some pieces of dry cake in his pack. It was his mother who'd baked the dry cake, sewn the little pack, and spun and woven the wool garments. His mother! When he'd asked for permission to ship out, she'd cried and his father had hidden himself in clouds of smoke from the cigarrette he was puffing: "It's an arm and a leg for us to see you go, but we won't keep you from a future you could never have here. Go, go on! And may God bless you!"

Francisco Marroco couldn't get to say goodbye to Maria because Roque had her under lock and key. When he was on his way out the door, going out into the night on the first step of his great journey through the World, he'd told his secret to his mother... And his mother had understood. And in the cold and the dampness which cut to his bones, the warmth of his mother's last kiss warmed his spirits.

João Peixe-Rei had left his wife racked with sobs. And his son, hands raised up to him, eyes smiling, surprised, not understanding! His son! And only for his sake was João leaving.

And so Francisco Marroco and João Peixe-Rei turned their eyes out toward the night-darkened sea. They didn't speak, they even feared to breathe, terrified as they were of the oarsmen. The waves whined, the breeze chilled them, the hours went by slowly.

Around midnight, they thought they saw a shadow on the water. Was it the longboat from the whaler? Was it the oarsmen's boat come to capture them? Didn't the government send the oarsmen to the Island just to keep an eye on the young men, just to keep them from shipping away and fleeing from the Island to the World?

"The bastards!" thought João Peixe-Rei bitterly.

He and his companion crouched lower, withdrew farther out of sight, their blood pounding in their veins, their hands grabbing onto the rough surface of the rocks.

Then the flicker of a weak light shone three times out on the water. Three times! That was the signal they'd agreed on. It was the whaler's boat come to take them off the Island!

Quickly they took out the flare and lit it three times and let themselves slip down through the rocks to the water's edge below.

And they found themselves among six stone-faced men, who received them without a word, without a gesture, and pulled at the oars in the silence of the night.

Besides the silence, there was only the light slapping of the oars and the whisper of the keel cutting softly through the dark waters.

And in Francisco Marroco's soul—the warmth of that kiss from his mother. And Maria, when she found out... Francisco Marroco felt something unknown, which he couldn't put his finger on, pressing hard on his chest. And João Peixe-Rei—he could *see* Idalina, her very white body overwhelmed by aloneness, by herself in the double bed. And the child, his boy—who would wait for him the next day, and the next one, and the ones after... And if he never saw his boy again!? Never!? Never ever!?

The Island was left astern, gone in the darkness of the starless, moonless night.

Ahead, they could make out the ship with its sails unfurled...

And the indifference of the men... (Real? Apparent?)

And the rocking of the boat...

And the phantom-like ship—the navigational lights hanging in the darkness—close, close, closer and closer...

And the thunk of wood against wood... The side of the boat knocking against the dark shape of the ship...

Francisco Marroco and João Peixe-Rei stayed on deck, leaning against the railing.

When the new day began, the first one of the two fugitives' journey through the World, the Island was nothing more than a grey cloud, outlined in the distance, like an upside-down funnel, back beyond the wake of the ship. Life on board was beginning again, and dozens of men were busy with their routine tasks. The captain was on the bridge, on the poop deck, talking to his lieutenant, to the mates, and checking the ship's compass for the course, asking the lookouts perched up on the mastheads sweeping the sea with their binoculars:

"No sign of whales? Keep a sharp eye, it's this time of year they're in these waters!" he advised, leaning against the balustrade, enjoying a look at the gulls which still flew over the mastheads, as if they too wished to flee the Island.

Francisco Marroco and João Peixe-Rei kept their eyes on him, hoping to get him to notice them, those strange fellows who'd asked him to take them on. And the captain seemed not to notice them.

One of the helmsmen came down from the bridge, up to Francisco Marroco and João Peixe-Rei, and spoke to them in English. When he saw they didn't understand, he called a mulatto who was swabbing the deck.

"You two, what're your names?" asked the mulatto in clear Portuguese.

"João."

"Francisco."

"Mine's António. Tony's what they call me here and I was born in Cape Verde. You'd better get yourselves American names. John... Frank... Come with me."

And he showed them their bunks in the forward compartments, and the boats, secured to the cranes by the poop deck.

"You, Frank, you'll be rowing in this boat, the first mate's. Yours, John, is that one, the second mate's." And then, seeing that Francisco Marroco didn't like the idea of being separated from his companion: "Don't worry, I'm the first mate's harpooner."

And he told them about his own life. He'd been around the World five times already, he'd been all over:

"One time, in the Pacific, our ship went to the bottom with more than half the crew. We made landfall, those of us who got to the boats, on a sandy island. We were there for more than seven months. Water—only from rain, and there were weeks without a drop of it falling. Food—only fish. There were twenty of us. When the ship which saved us arrived, six were left. But the sea puts a spell on people. Well, let's get to it. You, Frank, you're going to be in the galley, peeling potatoes. And you, John, come with me and swab down the deck."

João Peixe-Rei, seeing the captain nearby:
"I'd like to talk to the captain."
"Talk to the captain? Here, nobody talks to the captain unless he talks to you first. He gives all the orders, but through his lieutenant and the mates, and if we want something, we have to go to the mates.

"I'm going to the galley?" hesitated Francisco Marroco.
"*Yes.* Captain's orders. The cook's a Spaniard. You two will get along fine."

"The cook's a Spaniard!?"
"Yes, he is. And there are Frenchmen, Swedes, Englishmen, Russians, Indonesians. A hodge-podge of people. But we all live in peace." And with a sarcastic laugh: "There are also Americans. And, of course, the ship has to be American—the ship *Queen of the Seas,* out of New Bedford."

"*She blows!*" shouted the lookouts. "Windward! A pod!"

It was as if the ship had been struck by lightning. Carpenters, blacksmiths, the cook—the whole crew spilled out on deck, ran to the railing and shouted:
"*Blows! Blows!*"

The captain pushed the man at the helm away and took the wheel himself, roaring out, "Where are the whales?!"

"There, about six miles that way," pointed the lookouts.

The *Queen of the Seas* turned quickly to port, under full sail. Impatient, frenetic, the men could already see the whales' spouts, dozens of vapor trails, out in front, on the surface of the sea.

"*Blows! Blows!*"

Two miles from the pod, the sailors on the spars and the captain at the wheel took the steps necessary to bring the ship to a stop. Officers, harpooners, rowers went over the rail into the boats which were already in the water and rowed vigorously. The lieutenant's took the lead. The first mate's was still casting off.

"Frank! Jump!" bellowed Tony.

"Over here, boy!" And the first mate pointed out the midship's oar's bench to Francisco Marroco.

"No problem, Frank, don't worry," soothed Tony, seated at the bow oar, in his place as harpooner.

Standing in the bottom of the boat, steering it with his tiller oar, the first mate cursed and yelled to push the men on:

"At it, boys! Row, you son of a bitch, God forgive me! Row, you heaven's little angel. Row, you soul owned by the thirty thousand devils of hell, God forgive me! Row!"

Faces strained, teeth biting lips, the sailors put their oars to the water. Bodies and arms bent and pulled. They pulled the oars with all the strength of their muscles.

Francisco Marroco didn't understand the officer's words, nor his companions', for they were all spoken in English. But he could see the look on their faces and he heard Tony's encouragement:

"You can do it, son! You can do it!"

And so he rowed. He'd crack his bones, burst his heart, snap his nerves, but he'd be at his oar.

Behind, came the second mate's boat, with João Peixe-Rei at the second oar.

The three boats made their way forward to the pod of whales.

From the ship, binoculars to his eyes and watch in hand, the captain followed their progress. The few whalers still on board with him climbed up the masts, hung from the spars, and peered through the harsh morning sun. From their perches they too followed the boats and the whales. Each one used his own language, and they all put the fervor of the same prayer into their words:

"Just four more spouts. God help us spot it!"

And the boats got closer and closer to the whales. The officers, who were looking ahead, could see their bodies and their enormous heads break the surface and blow off steam. They wound the line around the loggerhead. It was more than four hundred meters of rope, played out from the tubs in the middle of the boat, toward the stern, wound two or three times around the loggerhead secured in the stern and fixed to the harpoon at the tip of the bow.

The lieutenant urged his men on:

"Come on, boys! One more stroke and we'll have our whale!"

And the first mate:

"Tony! Devil's soul, God forgive me! Get that harpoon for me! The lieutenant'll harpoon first. Thirty thousand devils take him, God forgive me!"

The captain looked at his watch, comparing the time until the whales sounded with the distance between whales and boats.

"They won't make it this time," he thought. "The whales have been up for a long time."

And the whales lifted their flukes and disappeared in white eddies.

"Damn them!" roared all the sailors.

"They're off to the devil!" roared the first mate.

"Listen-up there! Scan the whole ocean with your binoculars. They've got a good fill of air, and it might be far off they'll surface!" the captain ordered the lookouts, keeping his own eye peeled.

The officers noted on their watches the exact moment the whales sounded and brought their boats close to where they thought the whales would probably come up again. And about seven miles from the *Queen of the Seas,* the three boats, their oars ready, formed a large, approximately equilateral triangle. Standing on the benches, over the tillers, the officers watched. The sailors watched. Everybody smoked a pipe or cigarette, and some grumbled to themselves. The first mate said something which Tony translated for Francisco Marroco:

"He says you rowed like a *nice* whaler...

And Francisco Marroco, still shaky on his feet because they were not used to the boat's rocking, kept watch, too. His body ached—pains in his bones, in his flesh, in his numbed arms. His inexperienced eyes wouldn't recognize a whale, not even if it blew less than half a mile away. In reality, he didn't see boats, nor men, nor sea—but only the Island, in his heart, and his mother, and his father, and Maria.

He did, however, want to please the officer who, as he looked off into the distance, was thinking out loud:

"Twenty-five minutes... You people don't see any sign of the ship's masts? At least they've got their binoculars. Half an hour and three minutes... Whales in a pod should be coming up about now."

"*She blows!*" roared out Tony in the bow. "Here!"

"Pull hard, thirty thousand devils take it, God forgive me!" And with the tiller oar, the first mate set the boat on its way.

Francisco Marroco, encouraged by the praise he'd received, pulled at his oar, even though it felt as if his arms were being pulled from his body. The officer, biting his lip, eyes fixed on the whale spouts out beyond the bow, asked anxiously:

"The other boats?"

"They're far off," answered the rowers, still rowing.

"Tony! We'll be the first to sink a harpoon! Up with you and grab the harpoon!"

On board ship, the lookouts' thoughts were off bobbing along with the others' in the first mate's boat.

"Another blow and we'll have them," they whispered, holding their breath.

"That one there! The biggest one! Go for that one!" ordered the first mate.

And Tony, putting his whole body into it, cast his harpoon.

"Back up! Back up! Now!"

The line flew from stern to bow, between the men who were rowing back desperately. Only when they saw they were at a safe distance did they stop rowing.

And it was then that Francisco Marroco saw it. Crazed by the shock of the iron which had been embedded in its flesh, the whale tossed and turned up ahead. It was a fearful thing to see that black mountain throwing itself out of the sea, lifting its flukes, sweeping them from side to side, letting them fall in the tumult of the whitecaps churning as high as towers. Francisco Marroco was spellbound and nothing—not the boat, its crew, Tony, the first mate, the line—existed for him, except for the impact of the spectacle which surpassed whatever he had heard or could have imagined about it. Suddenly, he felt himself ripped from the immobility of surprise: one of his companions, eyes wide with fear, had just saved him from the line, which was playing out less than an inch from his legs. Pitching and rolling, the boat cut through mountains of white water behind the whale. Afraid of seeing the line disappear in the tubs—the heavy one was already completely played out—the first mate tried unsuccessfully to slip one more loop of line around the loggerhead. And when the whale, which had sounded, stopped pulling, there weren't even forty-five meters in the small tub. The men began to rewind: standing on the benches, indifferent to the burning midday sun, they recovered the played-out line by pulling it back into the boat.

Francisco Marroco, however, was still sitting. Pride, iron will, the wish to please the first mate, shock at the newness of the spectacle—everything was drained off by the weariness which weighed on him more heavily than the world. His oar resting across the gunnels, head nodding, arms hanging limp—his eyes closed on him, his mind clouded, his body went numb on him.

When the whale came out again, the first mate traded his place in the stern with Tony for his in the bow. It was the first mate's right to knife the beast, until he killed him with the iron of the lance. He gave the order:

"Row away from here! Heave to that side! Row on now, thirty thousand devils take it. Look alive, Tony!"

Tony didn't mind the bellowing of the first mate. A harpooner worth his weight in gold, he knew what he was supposed to do and handled the boat skillfully and surely. And noticing that Francisco Marroco was sitting still:

"Frank, get your oar into the water!"

With the lethargy which prostrated him, Francisco Marroco almost went unconscious.

"Get your oar in the water and row. Don't you see that..." Inside himself, Tony felt his impatience become splinters of anger.

The whale appeared larger near the boat. In the bow, standing, the first mate, lance in hand, body getting set to strike the blow, grumbled:

"Get closer, Tony! Even closer! Look alive, boys!" As he spoke, he pointed the lance at the flipper, straight at the heart and lungs of the animal. "Thirty thousand devils take it, God forgive me! Steady there with the boat! Now!" And he let fly the lance. "Back off now! Back off!" With the tip of the lance rope wound around his hands and his knees braced against the hull, the first mate yanked back the lance, which had gone deep into the whale's body.

Alertly, the rowers obeyed at once. With wide sweeps of the tiller oar, Tony saved the boat from the thrashing about of the desperate monster. He got angry with Francisco Marroco:

"Boy, you row or I'll break your head with the tiller shaft! None of us wants to be a cripple because of you!"

A revived Francisco Marroco looked over his shoulder and saw the whale there, flush with the bow. And, as if a hatchet blow had broken open the shell of his understanding, he realized he had to row, to contribute, with the help of his oar, to the salvation of them all. So he rowed, rowed so much that he was still rowing when the first mate had long since given the order to stop rowing. Tony was smiling:

"Man! Save your strength for later!"

The whale was still thrashing about some ways off. The whalers waited calmly for it to quiet down again.

And once more, the boat moved forward and the first mate sunk his lance in, and again the men rowed, and the boat was safe. Once, twice, three times, many times.

"It's spouting blood. It's here, it's dead," said the first mate.

And the boat moved off, moved off a good distance and stayed well back, the crew watching the whale, which was vomiting traces of squid and pieces of its own torn innards, which was spitting up, coughing up blood. All around, the sea was filled with blood. Afterward, the whale trembled, shook its head, threw up its flukes with an even greater effort than before, breeched completely out of the water. It fell back helplessly. It was dead. It must have been four in the afternoon. It had been harpooned at eight in the morning.

"Row forward 'cause we're going to take it in tow," ordered the first mate, now seated at the stern.

Sharks, their slim bodies and sinister eyes shining just under the water, appeared and rolled about in the water made red by the stuff which had been vomited, defecated and blown out by the whale in the last moments of its agony. When the boat was alongside its dead body, Tony, in the bow, leaning over the gunnel, used the spade to cut a hole in one of the flukes to thread the tow rope through. Meanwhile, the first mate was sizing up the whale with his experienced eye:

"At least that much...," acknowledged one of the rowers.

"Hold that boat steady," snapped Tony, "or it'll take us 'til tomorrow to get this whale in tow!"

And the first mate, giving a stroke with the tiller oar:

"It's like that whale off the Falklands..."

Since the whale had been hunted, harpooned and killed, the first mate became a loafer with figures, comparisons, stories about one whale or another, in the Pacific, in the Indian Ocean...

Standing in the bow, his hair hanging in his eyes, his arms wet up to his armpits, Tony ranted:

"Damn it to hell! Hold the boat steady. And you, cornhead (to a tousled-haired Swede), pass me that rope."

Annoyed, the first mate pulled on the tiller oar and ordered the oar by the tub to pull back, and paying more attention to the boat, continued:

"They were all about the same size in that pod. If all the others get lucky, we'll have around eighty barrels. Don't you see them?"

On the circle of closed sea on the horizon, nothing could be seen, except the *Queen of the Seas* in the distance, with her sails hanging limp in the still afternoon air.

Tony stood up, dried his hands on his trousers, used his right on his water- and sweat-soaked face, spread his fingers and buried them in his hair, running them back from his forehead:

"As far as I'm concerned, whenever you're ready. But until I eat, you won't get one single oarstroke from me."

The first mate opened up the cracker box and distributed the ration. The men chewed without a word. The keg came, too, and went from hand to hand. Each man lifted it, put the narrow slit of the neck to his parched lips and took just one swallow. Fresh water, even when bad, was worth its weight in gold—to wet the throat and wash down the bad taste.

Once hunger and thirst had been temporarily slaked, the first mate ordered them to take up their oars and begin to tow the whale. There were no clouds in the sky, and the sun was like a sinking fire on the horizon.

Francisco Marroco could barely pull his oar: if someone had put a hand over his mouth, he would have been snuffed out like the weak flame of a flickering candle. Tony felt sorry for him, spoke to the first mate and translated the answer:

"Frank! Put up your oar! Since it's your first time, the first mate says it's all right."

It was getting to be night. The stars twinkled in the sky. At a distant point on the surface of the water, lights on the masts and spars of the *Queen of the Seas* marked her location in the night. The boat couldn't make more than half a mile an hour—and, like slaves, the whalers rowed with their eyes fixed on those dots of light.

Francisco Marroco had fallen asleep, stretched out in the bottom of the boat. He was still sleeping like a log, curled up just like a dog at the feet of the officer when they tied up at the old ship, a little after midnight.

And the other boats were also coming in. The captain at the gangway directed the mooring maneuvers. He and the lookouts, eyes glued to their binoculars, had followed the fortunes of the hunt all day. When the first mate harpooned his whale, the others raised their flukes, hesitated for only a moment, and then left in a fright.

"They got scared," grumbled the whalers. If there's been enough of a breeze to get under sail..."

The heat burned and seared their skins, stifled their hearts. And the whalers rowed.

Small vessels, riding low in the water, three palms if that much, the boats disappeared from one another's sight. And the whalers, shackled to their oars, rowing all day.

And the whales, sensing their enemy near, went farther out, farther and farther out to sea.

"They're smart, those sons of bitches. All we're going to wind up with is the whale the first mate got," said the captain impatiently on board ship.

But the lieutenant and the second mate both managed to get their whales. They got back to the ship late, the second mate while the sun was poking its way through the clouds of a new day which was dawning sullenly.

With the furnace lit under the pots on the deck at midship, the *Queen of the Seas* spewed out billows of black smoke everywhere. And for many days, no one on board slept much at all.

Standing on the scaffolding hung over the side, each officer beheaded the whale his boat had harpooned and began to strip its body: he sunk in the spade, cut, tore and chopped.

The flensing was going on. Hooks on movable pulleys latched onto chains which were threaded through the stripped-off blubber. Thick, long ropes went up overhead through the fast pulleys on the mast, under the topsail, and wound the lead on the capstan, which the men, covered with sweat, were working. The tautened rigging creaked, the hull creaked, the ship listed. Enormous strips of white, shining blubber, encased in black, slid over the railing, hanging, twisted, in the air, and smacked onto the deck. Cut and re-cut, sliced and re-sliced, they were on their way to be boiled down to oil in the bottom of the pots.

The ship was a filthy slaughterhouse. The men seemed to have plunged into oil. In the sea, among patches of whitened fat and black spots of rotten gore, floated decomposing carcasses with their greenish guts swelling up in the sun.

The sharks gorged themselves. And while the ship, its decks well swabbed down and sails again unfurled, turned its bow to the routes of the South Atlantic, the sharks rolled in the muck left behind the wake of the *Queen of the Seas*.

Francisco Marroco and João Peixe-Rei didn't take long to understand: on board there was only one authority—total, indisputable, absolute, merciless, intransigent, unfeeling: the captain. Over him, only God.

Under the rigid discipline imposed by the authority there, there were no blacks, no whites, no Americans, no Frenchmen, no Russians, no Swedes, no Portuguese, no Spaniards. There, they were all whalers. Aside from being whalers, they were men—just men.

Isolated in the narrowness of that small world, which was dragging them over mysteries of the waters, they understood that one of them without the others was worth nothing. They kept their resentments, annoyances, ill-will to themselves, and each one was with the others and respected the others—their languages, their nationalities, their beliefs—so that the others would respect him, always accept him and never reject him.

His spirit and body toughened, Francisco Marroco had become a whaler—and a man—like any other. As for João Peixe-Rei, despite his easygoing ways, he showed himself ready right from the start for whatever came his way. The two began to understand and make themselves understood in the ragged English which was spoken on board. And they felt completely accepted by the others, to whom they had proved their understanding and solidarity during the tragedies and small joys which were part of life on board.

Every day, at dawn, the lookouts hoisted themselves to the heights of the masts. From time to time, they'd let out a cry that there was a whale in view. The boats left, they came back.

Sometimes, however, they were later than usual getting back. And there were those which returned with a cargo of bloody rags and bodies either dead or crippled for life. And there were those which made it back shattered and missing crew members. And those which the *Queen of the Seas* left behind after days and days of crossing back and forth between the four corners of the sea because the captain was certain they were irretrievably lost—either because a whale's flukes had smashed them or because they had gotten lost in a fog bank.

And with a shiver tearing at his guts, every whaler asked himself what his fate would be when the whales appeared again.

João Peixe-Rei was tortured by the idea that he might never see his son again. He'd had a bad dream. He found himself in a dark place, which he had never seen except in his dreams, and his boy was smiling at him nearby, in a patch of clear light, within reach of his hands. He was going to touch him, kiss him, hug him to his chest, let him feel his father's love and how much his father had missed him. Then something dark fell on João Peixe-Rei, smothering him, surrounding him, swallowing him up, strangling him, and he couldn't see his boy, who disappeared in the distance, smiling, still smiling.

And so, on they went over the saltwaters, all living the same life, and each one carrying along the other life that was his alone.

There were hurricanes and days with no wind at all. And then the thirst and hunger from the cutting back of rations because the ship was dragging along, delayed many weeks, many months by the torpor of tropical heat, or hindered by the whipping of shredded sails and broken masts. Meat covered with maggots, biscuits wrapped in mold, foul-smelling water. Scurvy was rampant, racking bodies, consuming lives. And still the lookouts climbed up to their perches at the tops of the masts. Yet, they were hoping to make out, beyond the spouts of whales, the silhouette of one of those apparitions which, with an immense column of smoke in place of sails, began to ply the seas with no need of favorable winds or ocean currents: so that the captain could beg the alms of green vegetables and fresh water to save them.

Of all the men who squeezed into the confines of the small world which was the *Queen of the Seas*, Tony must have been one of the few, perhaps the only one, who never lost his serenity, his good humor, his optimism. On nights graced with moonlight, he took up his guitar, sat out on deck, his legs crossed and his back against the foremast. His companions came and sat by him. On the bridge walked the captain, pipe in his mouth, hands buried in his pockets. The officers leaned over the railing. The man at the wheel kept his course by keeping his eyes on the compass.

The guitar moaned in Tony's hands, and his deep voice, tempered by winds and breezes from all the seas and lands of the World, wept in the soulful music and nostalgic lyrics of the sad *mornas* he had learned as a child on his island in the Cape Verdes. With cigarettes at their lips and eyes lost in the sea, which was covered in shimmering gold, the men sensed that their hearts wept in their chests. But it was a healthy, gentle, tender weeping.

Francisco Marroco saw, in the moonlight which reached his heart, his father with his guitar, Maria on that harvest night which had also been flooded with beautiful moonlight. And as he had the last time he saw her, he felt her hands in his, had the fire of her lips on his lips, the ring of the flesh of her arms around his neck. Then the tepid warmth of his mother's last kiss softly grazed his cheek. How much he missed her!

João Peixe-Rei remembered Idalina and, longingly, sometimes uncontrollably, her white body. And he remembered his boy.

The old ship bobbed along, marking time and gently rocking Tony's music, as if she, too, had feelings and dreams.

One of the mates came down from the bridge to say that the captain sent orders to turn in. Tony and his guitar fell silent, and the whalers, like quiet phantoms, slipped into the forecabin and lay down on their bunks.

From the ceiling, hanging from a beam, the rusty, smoke-stained lamp swayed back and forth, its weak flame the only light in the warm compartment. Francisco Marroco and João Peixe-Rei stared wonderingly at that flame. The Island, the village, America so far away...

"It seems to me that we've already been closer. Have you written home?" asked João Peixe-Rei.

"No. I haven't written for some time."

"We should write a letter to mail at the next port. I wonder what my boy's up to now. He must be getting pretty big."

"And my mother, my father, Maria..."

"As soon as I get to America"—João Peixe-Rei was fighting off the effects of the nightmare—"as soon as I can save some money, I'm going to send for Idalina and my Joaquim. In that great land, I'll make him into the kind of man who won't have to suffer what I've suffered. God won't turn me down on this one. That's all I ask of Him. Then I'll die happy."

"As for me, as soon as I can, I'll go back to the Island and marry Maria. And I want to take money, a lot of money for that rat Roque to see!"

By then, all the sailors were asleep, clothes unbuttoned, no covers on because it was so hot. The air they breathed was heavy and greasy with sweat, grime and body odor—the smells of a man who doesn't always get to take a bath. From time to time, a snort, a whistle, or a groan from those who snored scratched the silence.

Francisco Marroco and João Peixe-Rei, who'd long since gotten used to life on board, talked softly because they didn't want to wake anyone up. And little by little, they too fell asleep, still talking about the Island and the loved ones they'd left there.

Sometimes, in the middle of his sleep, João Peixe-Rei woke up, his flesh, his blood, his nerves tingling. He'd just held Idalina in his arms, her soul bound to his soul, her body clinging to his body. He'd be feeling about for the roundness of her breasts with his famished hands and for the warmth of her legs with his legs. He'd find only the narrow hardness and the cold boards of his bunk.

What he really feared was the nightmare, the bad dream which had torn his son from the love João Peixe-Rei felt as a father. Whenever he had the dream, he'd wake up terrified, in a cold sweat, and never get back to sleep. In the morning, he'd get up pale, sad, depressed. He'd move away from his companions and lean over the railing, his eyes open to the depths of the water and the foam around the ship.

Francisco Marroco asked:

"Are you sick, João?"

And Tony, with his friendly voice:

"John, what the devil's eating you? Get it out, man, it'll do you good!"

João Peixe-Rei shrugged his shoulder. He dreaded telling anybody about the dream for fear that if he did, something terrible would happen.

So the *Queen of the Seas* travelled the seas of the whole world, going to the Cape Verdes, Ascension, St. Helena, around the Cape of Good Hope, across the Indian Ocean, the Pacific—in short, to all the islands and regions of uncommon beauty.

When they made port at one of those ends of the World, right away there was the tiresome job of resupplying the ship, caulking the gashes in its hull, and repairing the masts and sails damaged from harsh temperatures, pounding waves, torrential downpours, the snows and the winds. Afterwards, there was time off from work and relief from the cruel journeys. Captain and officers lost themselves in whiskey and satiated their hungry flesh in the most expensive sporting houses. The sailors went ashore, farther, inland. They hung out with the seediest characters, satisfied their urge to get drunk in the worst dives and their need for love with the women who cost the least.

But now, since almost all the barrels they carried in the hold had been filled to the brim, they were on course for Cape Horn. It had been more than a week that they had been in a stinking calm; the sails hung on the masts without so much as a puff of air to fill them. The sun burned like molten lead, and the men were stretched out on deck, seeking the shade which they couldn't find. The lookouts would have been dozing on their perches were it not for the prodding of the captain and the officers.

It was the lookout on the mainmast who gave the alarm: "*She blows*!"

The boats fell into the water and the whalers, forgetting the heat, the fatigue, the nervous excitement, rowed hopefully. It was a large whale. With the oil it would produce filling out the cargo of the *Queen of the Seas*, they would set out on the surest course and the shortest route to New Bedford. They had been at sea for more than three years!

The whale sounded, surfaced, sounded again, surfaced again. It was the second mate who harpooned it.

The line ran out unrestrained and suddenly the officer shouted to the bow:

"Cut loose!"

Before the harpooner had time to cut, a man went overboard in a tangle of rope! They heard him as he went, choking in his struggle:

It was João Peixe-Rei.

(the land of America)

"Land ho!" yelled the lookouts.

The whalers all ran to the railing and looked and saw, shrouded in mist, out beyond the bow of the *Queen of the Seas*—the land of America!

Standing next to Tony, overwhelmed by the grief he felt inside for the death of João Peixe-Rei, Francisco Marroco also looked and also saw—the land of America.

"I know it's none of my business," Tony said to him, with some hesitation, "but do you have any money with you?"

"Any money?"

"Yes."

"How much money do you expect I'd have from home?"

"And where are you going to go looking for work?"
"California."
"It's a long way to California." And Tony's eyes turned away from Francisco Marroco's eyes. "It's on the other side of the country. To get there, you'll have to go all the way across the country. I don't know how many days by train. It's not cheap."
"Won't my share be enough?"
"You don't know that..." And Tony was silent.
"I don't know what?"
"That you're not getting a share?"
"I'm not getting a share!?"
"No. I thought you knew."
"And the money from my work?"
"The captain's hanging on to it, payment for dropping you off in America."
"That's not fair!" Francisco Marroco felt as if he'd been stabbed in the heart. "Nobody who ever left the Island the way I did even sent word back that that's the way things work!"
"And there're many other things they never sent back word about. No word back and they won't tell if they return. And you'll wind up doing the same thing."
"And what about João Peixe-Rei's share? Won't the captain send it to his wife after what happened?"
"Not at all."
"And what about her? Maybe you don't know how things are. A married man, poor the way João was, sets out in the World to make a better life. His family stays behind, living on credit, hoping to pay it all back when he sends some money. João's wife doesn't even know yet. I'm the one who'll have to tell her. And, as for the money, she might even think that I pocketed her husband's share."

It was getting on to night. In the distance, luminous

clouds hovered over the earth.

"Tomorrow, stick with me when we go ashore." And Tony took a drag on the cigarette he had lit.

Moved by what he had heard, he spoke to his companions and appealed to their unselfish and generous sense of understanding and human solidarity.

...And the money Tony collected from the crew of the *Queen of the Seas* Francisco Marroco enclosed with the letter he sent from New Bedford to Idalina, along with one for his parents and one for Maria. They also paid his train ticket to California and gave him a few dollars to keep him from starving for the first few days.

Francisco Marroco had spent the last cent a long time ago and was wandering the roads of California, hungry, when he found work in the San Joaquin Valley, on the farm belonging to Albano Passarinho, an Azorean from the Island of São Jorge.

It was a very large farm, and if the men had worked like human beings, Albano Passarinho would have needed ninety to one hundred workers. He got along with forty, fifty. And there was plenty of seed to sow in the fields, the harvests were good, the cattle were always fat. He enjoyed making those who worked for him pay for the affronts he had suffered in silence and with downcast eyes at the hands of the bosses he had worked for. He rationalized: with his sweat, he had made the rich richer. Now, since he too was wealthy, there could be nothing more fitting than for the poor to work to make him richer. And anyone who stepped out of line or got sick could hit the road: "My place is not a flophouse for bums." And that said it all.

Even so, he was never short of people to work for him. The world poured many, many people into the American EL DORADO, people who came willing to do anything and bent their necks to the yoke of servitude.

Albano Passarinho received Francisco Marroco with open arms. From the Azores, was he from Pico?! Yes, sir, he remembered. When he was a boy, from his village, Toledos, he wondered at the size of the mountain, from across the channel. Then, he'd realized that it was nothing compared to the mountains of America. Why, there wasn't a land bigger, prettier, richer than America. The Azores! People shouldn't even be living on those rocks! And he rambled on, turning over in his mind the dream he'd had a thousand times and whose realization he'd put off just as often: to go back to the Island, dazzle his relatives and friends with the spectacle of his wealth and smooth-talk the prettiest girl into rubbing his callouses and sweetening up his coming old age. And he tried to encourage Francisco Marroco:

"You're a kid. Here, anybody who's young can get rich, except if he doesn't try. What he has to do is work and obey the bosses. You can work for me, if you like. I pay half a peso a day. If it'll do."

Why wouldn't it do?! Francisco Marroco was really grateful!

And, anxious for news from the Island (because of his wanderings, he'd heard nothing from home since he left), he decided to write his parents and his girl friend. But because it wouldn't look good for the *americano* who sent it for the letter to arrive empty, nor for the family receiving it, he got Albano Passarinho to give him an advance. Folded up with the letter, the bill would fool his family and his friends.

And he worked. And the difficult working conditions drained his body and soul. He got up before there was light through the keyhole of the shack the workers used as a bunkhouse and he went to bed after midnight. He and all the others.

He was terribly homesick and counted the days, waiting for letters.

One night, he had gathered a sheaf of alfalfa for the horses and was on his way to the stable when he heard:

"Come with me." It was the voice of the boss, who'd gone round the barns, checking up after his hands, and was going up the stairs to the porch in front of his house.

Surprised and frightened, Francisco Marroco followed Albano Passarinho. He'd been working for him for seven months and had gotten to know him. He'd seen him fire many workers for no apparent reason. He didn't consider himself any more special than anyone else. He couldn't work any harder than he did. No matter how much he turned things over in his mind, he couldn't think of anything he'd done wrong and his conscience was clear. But Albano Passarinho was the boss: as far as he was concerned, he could choose anyone he wanted. And Francisco Marroco was consumed by possibilities.

"Come in!" Albano Passarinho disappeared through the doorway and came back with a letter: "It came today."

Francisco Marroco didn't need to touch or look at the letter to know it was from his parents... from Maria. He forgot the cows, the horses, the sheaf of alfalfa. He flew down the stairs, ran across the yard, slipped into the shack, lit the oil lamp on the makeshift table made of old boards—and opened the envelope.

My dear, dear son:

It's more than four years you've been gone from us and since then there's been no joy in this house because you were our joy well we got your letters you sent us from those places out there in the world and the two you sent after you got to that blessed land of America and your money but you didn't

> *have to because well I passed on the letters you sent us for Roque's Maria and I gave the message you left the night you went off going on four years she poor thing was still kept at home in that house her father shut her in like she was in prision and she still didn't know and then she was like family had died on her and she took up living like a widow she only goes out to mass on Sundays and nobody sees her anymore not even at the feasts of the Holy Ghost don't ever forget her remember how ashamed I've been to be a go-between and I never was good at it and your father doesn't like it either but you are our heart's own son and she gave me a note I'm sending along here...*

Anxious, Francisco Marroco went through the sheets of paper, searching. It was the last one, Maria's letter.

> *Dear love of my heart*
>
> *This morning I met up with your mother who gave me the letter you sent saying you were working on a farm and I'm answering right away 'cause your mother said she was going to write today and I don't want you to get a letter from her and not from me. It's a short letter 'cause I'm afraid my father might catch me. I also got the letters you sent before and I didn't answer 'cause nobody knew where you were. You could've told me, my love, that you were going off like that since you'd decided anyway and I would've waited, but I'd rather have you poor and never be an americano than for you to be living far away and having a bad time of it across those salt waters in those lands*

> *that are not our land. But you left me and you don't even know what I've suffered always thinking about you afraid something'll happen to you, dear love, like it did to João Peixe-Rei. It's just as well you're in America and me, I'll wait back here. I'm a widow and I've never been married, but I'm happy to be able to miss you. My father hasn't changed his mind, but my mother is on our side, poor thing, she's the one who goes to the shop to take these lines to your mother who's agreed to meet her. And I can't stay any longer, good-bye, dear love of my heart, take the kisses and hugs sent by this one who promises to be yours until death and misses you so much that only seeing you will do.*
> *O X O X O X O X O X O X O X O X O X O X O X O X O X O X O*
>
> *Maria*

Francisco Marroco kissed that scrap of paper and the O's and X's that were Maria's hugs and kissees. He went back to reading his mother's letter:

> *...well my dear son what happened to João Peixe-Rei was the worst you could think of it was the end of the world in Idalina's house when your letter came and his little money couldn't help much and maybe not even enough to pay in the shop for the corn she's been buying and she just isn't the same always keeping inside the house with that child poor kid and his father never had a good job and never got to take him away from here he looks to be very smart he's in school and the teacher says she's never had any other child as alert and they say*

his father left for his sake and was lost at sea and it looks like punishment from God who doesn't want the poor to stop being poor because my dear son here we had a very long drought the year you left it didn't rain till September it was sad to see what happened to the corn what helped was the boatload Manuel Ratinho had sent from that blessed land and gave free to the people and he didn't make any money at all but some tried to give him a hard time the people from Piedade came with Father Mouco to take the corn they wanted and Manuel Ratinho said they'd get some but first it was for the people by the inlets and they tried to take all the corn by force before the rest got their share but our people stopped them and they went off yelling and screaming and Father Mouco used to having his own way marched off to Faial to tell the government that Manuel Ratinho was giving away corn to buy votes and bring down the king and set up a republic and the next day the gunboat came and arrested Manuel Ratinho and the people didn't really want to let it happen and they came to the pier the men with sickles and scythes and the women with stones under their skirts to keep the sailors and soldiers from laying a hand on Manuel Ratinho but he got up on the rocks behind the pier and made a speech I wish you could've heard telling us to think of our children and for the men not to settle things by force and the people to calm down and let them take him because nothing would happen to him he almost made the people cry and the rocks too and he got them to stop and off he went to Faial and he told the government there what needed to be said he talked about the poor here without anything to eat and abandoned and he asked if they wanted things to happen the way they did in the Year of the Famine well he also got the people of Faial in the government house who came to see this man who wanted to kill the king from Lisbon but I don't know where Lisbon is and the civil governor was also moved and saw things his way and sent him back here and soldiers to help him do what he wanted to do and when he set foot on the pier we had a celebration like our village had never seen and we got corn and there was enough for everybody I hope Our Lord will always remember Manuel Ratinho if he hadn't been there it would've been like it was in the Year of the Famine the way your grandfather told about it when some cows and pigs died and our fine pig died and you were the one who had gone to sell it at Rangana's house at your father's order and after that we never killed any because without you here with us it hasn't been the same and this is a sad house and your father's tired out and he hasn't laid hands on his guitar which is still hanging in the front room on a nail next to the clock getting covered with dust and cobwebs well at first people still asked him to play it at parties and he turned his head away so they wouldn't see him cry and then they stopped coming and I too am getting old and my son it's good you're working with people from our Islands that's some consolation and I hope to God we're still alive when you come home to get married well my son I don't remember if I already told you that Captain Silvestre ordered another boat which they call the big boat and the officer was master Luís and with the second whale he harpooned he got his leg tangled in the line and it got torn right off his body and it was a day of judgment in this village and some of the others who died since you left are Ti Joaquim Bacalhau and Triana's Francisco and Rita's António and Vicente Pau André's Maria Inácio Mamão and Anjinho's Ti Filomena poor thing she suffered a lot at the end and she was so nice with her white bread soup with coffee with sugar cubes and those mean people she'd helped all treated her badly oh well we never know what's to be our lot son this month of August there hasn't been any rain but God's will be done well I don't want to bore you any longer never forget God and Our Lady and all the saints and our patron saint Sebastião and show respect for people and your bosses and tell the truth and don't do bad things we're poor people but we've always been true and polite and I'm sorry to be going on like this but you're our son and as long as you are we have to give you our advice good-bye my soul's own son your friends and Tia Angelina and Manuel Pimpão and your cousins and aunts and uncles all say hello and here's a big hug and blessings from your father and your mother

Isabel

Francisco Marroco sat there with the letters dangling from his hands, which felt as heavy as fetters on his knees. His eyes, which were blind to the real world around him, could see, through the cloud of his tears, only the world he carried inside him. He wasn't aware of his companions, who came in and threw their exhausted bodies on the beds which were lined up next to each other along the walls. He didn't hear them snore, he didn't hear the wind which rolled over the roof with the purr of a contented cat, not the whinny of the horses, nor the lowing of the cows outside in the stables and barns. He paid no mind to the passage of time and his arms dropped to the table and his head onto his arms, lids closed over his eyes. The light of the oil lamp bit by bit became the flame of the lamp hanging from the beam in the kitchen of his parents' house.

Francisco Marroco *was* there, on the Island, in his parents' house, sitting on the mat in the kitchen, on a Winter's night. The sea, the wind, the rain... The neighbors were coming in for the evening's festivities, his father was smoking, the guitar moaning in his hands, his mother was darning, his grandfather was telling sad stories, Maria, very pretty, appeared there, too.

He felt someone shaking him and calling. His mother, of course. But that hoarse voice and those rough hands...

He opened his eyes. The flame in the oil lamp was going out. His companions were dragging themselves like ghosts. They opened the door and went out in the darkness.

Still groggy, his heart overflowing with bitterness, his body worn-out, his eyes aching in their sockets, Francisco Marroco slipped the letters into his back pocket and followed the others out to face another day's work. It was four o'clock in the morning.

As he was going into the barns, he bumped into Albano Passarinho.

On his last round, Albano Passarinho had come upon the forgotten sheaf of alfalfa on the ground and the horses without their rations. With barely a word, he paid Francisco Marroco for his time and told him to go find work somewhere else.

Out in the cold again, with only his bedroll and the

clothes on his back, on America's seemingly endless roads, Francisco Marroco passed through cities, towns, villages; he went from door to door, offering the services of his body's strength—a piece of merchandise to be given, even if for only a crust of bread, to the first buyer who accepted it.

"Maybe up the road a way," people would tell him and they'd move on because no one had the time nor the patience to help out other people.

He ran into those who were going around, like himself, in search of work in the land of America—and into the tramps, whom he avoided because he'd heard the worst things about them.

And he kept on his way. The bedroll was very heavy on his back and his feet hurt and his boots were worn-out.

He always got the same answer: "Further on, maybe a bit further on."

The little money he'd received from working for Albano Passarinho was soon gone. The notion of going hungry terrified him. He settled down to eating twice a day and sleeping out in the open, leaning against walls and trees.

Winter came. Rain fell, snow fell. At night, he took shelter in tramps' refuges: in run-down shacks with no doors, no windows, roof falling in, and in railroad stations on the outskirts of towns. He'd enter unsure, feet feeling their way through the packed-in bodies, wrap himself in his covers and settle into the corner which seemed the most comfortable. Those places reeked with humidity, with rags and bodies stained by the sweat and dust of long journeys and sufferings. Sometimes, a fire with suffocating smoke furnished light and warmth. The hobos talked, they seemed to preach—and Francisco Marroco covered his head so he would not hear them. Desperately trying to deny the realities of his situation, if someone made a friendly overture, his flesh crawled, with waves of nausea. He held back any word of acknowledgment, any handshake, any expression of feelings of understanding (in his pocket, he still had a few nickels and still bought food, although lately he'd been down to eating once a day). And before daylight, he was back out on the road.

Then, when his last cent was gone, Francisco Marroco would beg for handouts from the rich, and when they turned him down and he couldn't stand the hunger any longer, he'd rob scraps from the dogs which rummaged around garbage cans and snatch fruit hanging from trees along the roadsides. He had lost his earlier confidence, his faith in the American paradise and the justice of men (despite his memory of Tony and his companions on the *Queen of the Seas)* and he hated: Captain Grilo, Albano Passarinho, the dogs he couldn't always beat out for the scraps, the men who'd occasionally give him something to eat, lucky because they had a chance to be generous, and those who refused him work—which he wanted as his right and not as charity.

He felt himself beaten down. Every day it got harder for him to beg. The bedroll was crushing him. His feet, covered with blisters, raw, hurt him. And he kept on.

And at night, very far from the shack or the train station yard of the night before, he would fall in with other tramps in another shack or another station. His eyes no longer turned from theirs. He no longer rejected them; now he listened to them; he took part in the conversations with which they joined together in human warmth during the freezing nights. And when he was making his way alone along inhospitable roads, he missed the night and the company of the tramps as he would the warmth of family.

Among them could be found boys like Francisco Marroco who'd left the poverty of their native lands, whose eyes had gleamed with the spark of dreams and hope, sure that it wouldn't be long until they made their fortunes and found their happiness. But reality was otherwise, and they suffered shock after shock. They took to one deception after another, perhaps destined to wind up in the morass of organized crime after all.

And with those were the ones who attacked the exploitation of man by man with revolt and faith in their ideal of justice and human redemption. In cities and towns, he heard the prophets of that New World and at night in the shacks and stations, they themselves preached the good news. And Francisco Marroco listened carefully to their words:

"Slavery was abolished," they said. "We are men and not animals."

They explained that they accepted the obligation to work because they maintained that those who refused to work had no right to life and bread. They would, however, never abdicate their rights as free men. Pioneers of the New World, some of them soldiers in the crusade which freed the slaves of the South, they were going forward in the great battle for the freedom of Man. And it tore their hearts out to see freedom ravaged in the land of America. Lincoln had been assassinated. The rich still imposed slave labor with no protections. And they got excited.

"But we are alive! If we unite and stay off the job under the existing arbitrary conditions, they will have to hear the rightness of our justice! They have their money—we have the labor of our arms and hands! Labor can survive without money—money cannot live without labor! With just our labor, we can build cities, even in the sands of the desert, or we can bring down nations. Let us unite! And let us refuse ourselves intransigently—although for this we might lose our lives! Until all are convinced that it shall never be right for man to prey on his fellows!" And, as if in a dream: "The accumulation of property in the hands of the few at the expense of the many shall not be in the New World. Land and Industry shall be the property of the people—so that all may freely enjoy the benefits of their products. If not, man would spend his life working only to end up with no place to drop dead."

Francisco Marroco drank in the words of the visionaries, although he didn't understand all of them, nor did he agree with everything. There were, however, those who continually grumbled about the haranguing which kept them from sleeping. They were the permanently down and out. With no ideal, arms inactive and spirits crushed, the act of stretching out a hand in the unworthy gesture of begging or stealing did not turn their stomachs, put their nerves on edge, bother their consciences. Some of them would end up hanging from a gallows.

And at dawn all those people seattered at random over the highways that criss-cross the American land.

Once more, dryly and briefly, Francisco Marroco repeated:

"I want work."

And he waited for the words everyone used to chase him away: "Maybe a bit further on up the road."

That was not, however, what he heard from the man with the friendly smile on his face:

"Are you American?"

"No."

"European?"

"From the Azores."

The man was moved and spoke the sweet Portuguese language:

"What island?"

"Pico."

"You know Terceira?"

"When I used to go to the woods, when the weather was clear, sometimes I'd see Terceira in the distance, beyond São Jorge."

"That's my land, Terceira. I'd like to end my days there: on my land, in the house where I was born. But come in, come in. You must be really hungry. We were just getting ready to eat."

And he announced to everyone in the house with a joy he couldn't keep to himself: "Elisa! Elisa! Somebody from back home! Somebody from the Azores!"

They crossed the hall and were received in the kitchen by the kindness of a woman who was still young, the smiles of three children, the soft warmth of the lamp's flame, the bounty of the well-set table.

"He's from the Azores, from Pico!" repeated the man to his wife, his eyes shining. And then to Francisco Marroco: "This is my family. My wife, my children. Elisa's from the Azores, too. From Graciosa."

The woman spoke, and in her words, there was as much excitement as in her husband's:

"You left there a long time ago?"

"Yes, a long time ago. I went whaling. I worked for Albano Passarinho."

"That wasn't your luckiest experience. I was here no more than a half dozen years when he came. Today, he's worth more than half a million. I bought this farm just two years ago, it's no big thing, and I haven't paid for it completely yet. I don't have his guts. But let's eat." And the man sat down at the end of the table in his place as head of the family. "Sit down, sit down and eat."

The children stayed to one side, quiet, still, studying the stranger. The mother chided them, as part of her responsibility as housewife:

"Charles, Edna, Rose! Mind your manners! Go sit down at the table and say hello."

"That's right, come to think of it," inquired the man, "you haven't told me your name..."

"Francisco. Francisco Marroco. Here they call me Frank."

"Myself, my name's Miguel Parreira. Please make yourself at home. From Terceira, I could see Pico, the mountain's peak over the hump of São Jorge, and the far end of it south of Topo..."

Francisco Marroco couldn't believe what was happening to him. He was eating, feasting, stuffing himself, strangling that old hunger which burned away at his insides. He was even afraid they'd think something was wrong, he was so hungry.

Miguel Parreira understood:

"Eat, Francisco, eat! Anybody who's been on the road for long is bound to have a belly which won't let him forget he's hungry. Just remember I also travelled the roads of America looking for work!"

"Go on! Have some more beans! We'll have no pretending," insisted Elisa.

The youngest of the children had lost her shyness and climbed up on Francisco Marroco's knees. She looked in wonder at his heavy, dirty whiskers and marvelled at his huge appetite.

And for the first time since he'd left his family, Francisco Marroco felt the welcome of a home.

There he stayed, treated like a son, with his place at the table and his bed underneath the same roof which sheltered the others. A fair man, Miguel Parreira increased his pay from time to time as the crops and income from the cows permitted. And he suggested in a fatherly way:

"Get your life in order. Be careful with your money because you never know what might come up."

And in the Winter during the nights made long by cold and homesickness, they gathered in the kitchen, around the fire, Miguel Parreira puffing on his pipe, Francisco Marroco smoking a cigarette, Elisa sewing or ironing. They spoke about the Islands, they read the letters they'd received, they imagined what their relatives were doing, they planned the return they always put off. And Elisa noted with her sharp sense of realities:

"We have to end our days here. We can go to the Azores, but not to stay. Our children's country is here—and our children's country is also our country."

Her husband let his head fall, the dream of ending his days in the house where he'd been born crumbling inside him.

The children heard their parents and Francisco Marroco.

Charles had become a man and, refusing to go to college, was another pair of arms available to contribute to the peace and prosperity of the farm. The girls, young women of marrying age, were finishing up high school.

One of those nights, Miguel Parreira said to Francisco Marroco:

"I heard in town that a farm nearby here will be up for sale soon. Might be what you're looking for. You have a few dollars. We'll be sorry to see you go, but..."

No. For the time being, Francisco Marroco would not buy a farm. First, he'd go to the Island, to get married. Then, well, if he came back...

Miguel Parreira was wrapped in the smoke from his pipe, quiet. Go to the Island to get married... Weren't his daughters right there, closer? And to have Francisco Marroco as a son-in-law wouldn't make him unhappy. But that was something he kept to himself.

"Well, if it's because you're going back to the Island to get married," he said, "a loan can be arranged. You leave after you buy the farm and you bring your wife back here to your land."

Francisco Marroco was afraid of loans.

And so the letters came, filled with gloom and longing, always two of them, one from his mother or father, the other from his beloved.

> *...we're no good for anything anymore Francisco (this time it was his father who wrote) this is a sad house and when I go through the front room by our guitar I feel a tug at my heart reminding me of when I saw you dancing with Roque's Maria and one day I took the guitar down from the hook cleaned off the cobwebs and dust and strummed the rusty strings and it sounded like a split reed not like the instrument which used to play at so many parties your mother came in and we fell into each other's arms crying with the grief of everything and missing you we're two old boats at the end of their journey in the stormy sea of life the miles are counted land's in sight and what we most want Francisco would be to see you while we're still here...*

And in Maria's letter:

> *...always wait for you, my love, I watch the clouds and the stars in the hope that they've seen you in those lands where you are and I look at the ships hoping they bring news of you or that you're on one of them, but the news takes a long time to get here and you never come. I get to the point of hating the sea which opened a road to the World for you, but then I feel sorry because only the sea can bring you back to the warmth of my arms and my kisses. And I ask it to bring you, but it's deaf and never hears me. And in the afternoon when the*

sun goes down and the land and the sea are different, I begin looking at the stones on the roads, the grass, the trees, the woods along the paths where you used to walk and then I feel like kissing everything and I stand there waiting for you to appear, dear heart, the way you used to. I live waiting for you...

Francisco Marroco started when he realized how many years had gone by. He was over thirty, he was getting on in years, and he had been with the Parreiras for more than a dozen.

Alone in his room, he opened the drawer of his bedside table, took out his bankbook and added up the deposits: fifteen, almost sixteen thousand dollars, a sizeable amount for the time.

Why not go back? If it did not take too long to get ready, he would arrive in the Spring, around the time of Pentecost.

That evening, he showed the letters to Miguel Parreira and Elisa, who found his silence and the expression of his face unusual.

"I've decided to go," he announced, when he saw they'd finished reading.

Charles, Rose, Edna followed the gestures, silences and words of Francisco Marroco and their parents. They insisted on knowing:

"But where are you going?"

Elisa got up. Her husband was wrapped in the smoke from his pipe:

"I think you're doing the right thing," he said. "We're the ones who can't go."

"But where's Francisco going?" demanded the children.

"To the Island!"

They all stood around him, enclosing him in their longtime friendship.

"For good?"

The light from the lamp lit up the faces of the six people.

Francisco Marroco did not know. He was going to see his parents and get married. He would leave his money in America. Afterward he would decide.

PART TWO

RETURN

(feast day—Pentecost Sunday)

He left California one night in April when the sky was calm and shining with stars.

Spitting up smoke and banging against the iron rails, the train began to move away, slowly at first, then more quickly; and at one of the windows in his third-class car, Francisco Marroco said good-bye to his friends, Miguel Parreira, his wife and their children who, with moist eyes, waved little white handkerchiefs from afar, farther and farther away.

He sailed from New York on the transatlantic ship *Canopic*, which took him to São Miguel, and he arrived at the Island on the sailboat *São Joaquim* the morning of Pentecost Saturday.

And when he set foot on Pico...

Body and soul bent over in sobs, Francisco Marroco fell on his knees and kissed those dark stones with his lips as he moistened them with his tears. And he held tightly to himself the trembling body of his father, the frail body of his mother, the straining body of Maria. And it was the same with the relatives and friends who showed up.

Then his trunks were opened—and his father, his mother, Maria, his relatives, his friends stood amazed at the things which filled the house with the smell of America. They all wanted to see and feel those treasures for themselves.

At night, there was music and it settled in the tight little room and filled the people-packed house with joy.

It was only in the early morning when all was quiet that Francisco Marroco and Maria could finally be alone. They fell into each other's arms, holding on to each other ever so tightly.

The next day—feast day—Pentecost Sunday!

Blue sky, blue sea, bells ringing, firecrackers going off, music playing!

The procession went by with the revelers in front beating on their drums when the music stopped—bang-bang-a-bang, bang-a-bang-bang-bang—beating and singing:

> *And our Lord Holy Ghost*
> *Up the hill, up he comes!*
> *To help the majordomo*
> *Shake the sifter!*

The revelers and right behind them the damask banner, the majordomo with a red sash across his chest, the queen dressed in white, a golden diadem on her brown hair and the silver crown in her brunette's hands. And children with bouquets of flowers, the musicians with their white uniforms and shining instruments, the line of the "brothers" dripping sweat in their Sunday suits, alongside the girls carrying flowered baskets on their heads, full of cakes made the night before.

In the church, which is flooded with light and scents, the queen kneels so the priest can crown her—and in the choir-loft, the voices of the singers tremble. The whole church is in song, everyone's spirit sings!

And in the courtyard, that afternoon, the euphoria of the whole population. Flags flying, young men and women strolling and courting—the men offering sweets, the women returning smiles. And fireworks, and music.

At the corner of the atrium, Francisco Marroco looked at his father and he looked at his mother. And he looked at the fields and at the sea belonging to that lovely land (he had never imagined it so lovely) which was his land. And he looked at Maria. Maria's black hair, her dark-complexioned face, her black eyes shining and smiling, her full, red lips, her well-formed bust with full breasts held high, her slim waist, her rounded hips and at the hem of her skirt, the flash of her leg.. Maria! All of that was Maria!

His lips did not speak, nor did hers, for it was only their bodies close together, their intertwined hands, their souls seen in their eyes which did...

The old, the young, men, women and even children, all of them marvelled at Francisco Marroco: his fine suit, his shining shoes, his splendid necktie, the gold chain across his front, the watch tucked into his vest pocket, the ring around his finger. And his father and mother, his father-in-law and mother-in-law (soon-to-be because old Roque had forgotten his obstinacy of times gone by) all dressed up in new outfits. And Maria—whom no one had ever seen without a shawl over her head—totally happy, in silk clothes, earrings in her ears, necklaces around her neck, rings on her fingers. And all those clothes, those trinkets and all those luxury items on the old folks and on Maria—brought from America by Francisco Marroco, the senhor americano!

And there came the "brothers" of Pentecost Sunday, offering everybody glasses of local wine and cakes.

Relatives, friends, acquaintances came with embraces

and best wishes for Francisco Marroco, who, as the *americano,* spoke up:

"Let's go have a drink because I want to make a toast!"

And off they went, a happy crowd, to Master Augusto Bóia's place. On his way back, Francisco Marroco was bringing packages of sweets—of the sort that courting men offer their ladies, on such a day.

"We're also courting." And he gave Maria the sweets he'd bought only for her.

The fireworks went off, the music played. Already the evening was showing the serenity of the sky and the sea. A shadow overcast and saddened Francisco Marroco's soul: João Peixe-Rei. He had not yet seen his widow, nor his son.

"What's happened to Idalina?" he asked Maria. "Idalina and the boy?"

"Poor things! They didn't have anything to wear to the feast."

"I have to find them."

As they burst in air, the skyrockets were stars which instantaneously shone in the sky. The orchestra was playing the last numbers, the lovers were on the last turn of their stroll, exchanging words and vows of love...

But night had fallen and for Francisco Marroco the night was painful with the memory of João Peixe-Rei.

(the presence of his friend
buried in distant waters)

Francisco Marroco walked through the latchless doorway, opened in the half-crumbling wall, crossed the short patio, went up the half dozen stairs which led into the kitchen porch. It was run-down, lonesomely dark, with a warped roof and glassless windows, that house which at another time, in the Spring, João Peixe-Rei had spruced up and whitewashed. There were no hogs, no chickens, no goats in the pen. The garden walls were almost in ruins.

He knocked at the hole-filled door, and a cat ran out from under it. Without waiting, he knocked a second and a third time and heard the bare feet of someone who'd just gotten up. An old woman appeared—white hair, shrunken face, bent back, withered body, raggedy clothes—and made only a gesture for him to go in.

If it weren't for a few traces of light in her eyes, no one would have seen in the poor thing the beautiful Idalina whom João Peixe-Rei had loved.

For a few moments—arms at their sides, hands limp, eyes aching in their sockets—they stood facing each other without a word. Then, overwhelmed, racked with sobs, she threw her arms around Francisco Marroco.

"Francisco, my dear Francisco, you've come back to our land! But my João..." She could not speak, her body was shaking so.

Just inside the door which opened onto the interior of the house, there appeared a young man of about twenty. He was short and frail, in bare feet and without a shirt on, and was buttoning up his trousers indifferently and quietly.

"'My son! This man is Mr. Francisco, your father's friend!" And from the midst of more sobbing: "Oh, João! Poor man! So many years since he left never to return! It seems only yesterday. I can see him saying good-bye to us that night when you two slipped away. How much I and this boy here have suffered since we got that letter you sent. They say that losing your mother is a bad thing. Maybe so. But to lose your father!... A father's breath is enough to command respect, even if he's far off and away." She calmed down a bit: "But, come, sit down, Francisco." And she went looking for a chair she didn't have.

"Don't bother, Idalina."

The young man, a gloomy look on his face, leaned against the fireless hearth, and Francisco Marroco sat down on the floor, where the young man had been.

"You can't imagine what I and my son, Joaquim, have been through!"

At a very young age and quickly, Joaquim had learned to understand, form and put together the letters of the alphabet, to join figures to get numbers and to carry out the four operations of arithmetic with ease.

"Few minds like this one have been in my class," the teacher had praised him. "Once something's been taught to him, he never forgets it!"

The mothers of other students heard her and whenever they saw her at the church door after Sunday mass or during gossip sessions at the crossroads:

"And your boy? God bless him! I just wanted you to hear about how much the teacher misses him! Be careful, don't let anyone put the evil eye on him because some people are capable of anything and there's more of them to do bad than to do good. And your husband? Any word? Has he made it to America?"

Idalina wasn't ignorant of the amount of envy behind those honeyed words nor of what was said openly behind her back. Even so, the reality of the envy itself made her proud. Her son was the best student in the school and soon her husband would begin sending dollars, and she, sooner or later, the wife of an *americano,* would become the mother of a priest or a scholar. If God and the Virgin didn't let her down...

At night, before going to bed, she leaned on the bedpost, knelt before the holy pictures on the wall and taught her son to pray:

"Fold your hands, Joaquim! We're going to pray for those who are off at sea. We're going to pray for your father. Our father, Hail Mary..."

Joaquim barely remembered his father. Still he sort of missed him, felt a hazy affection for him, an undefined respect for that father who'd gone off, sailed far away in distant mists and would return, someday.

On windy Winter nights, the sea smashed against the coast, the wind shook doors and windows. Joaquim didn't want his father to return on one of those nights. Instead he hoped to see his father come back on a moonlit night or on a day shining with sun. And in bed, under the covers, he snuggled into the arms of his mother, who put out the light, stretched out next to him and, unable to sleep, shivering with the blast of the storm, kept on praying to Our Lady of the Sailors...

But then came Francisco Marroco's letter. The village came to the funeral mass which she had said for her dear departed one, and they all joined their conventional laments to the grief of the unfortunate widow:

"Poor dear! And your boy? Don't take him out of school!"

Joaquim understood his mother's pain and he suffered, although he couldn't say how he felt except with many silent tears. It was that father, whom he barely remembered, who would never be back again!

Life became gloomy and hard for the two of them. With the money which had come with Francisco Marroco's letter, Idalina paid what she owed and few were the coins she had left over. Soon after, if she wanted to buy fish, corn, a few coppers of soap, or a snatch of calico, the same people who up until then had insisted, "Here, take it, it won't be long before you'll have money from America," those same people now were saying, before a sale, "Things are so expensive.

Things are in bad shape." Sensing she had no money left, they never again sold her anything at all on credit.

Idalina could have given up—but she struggled. She knocked at the door of the priest, the teacher, the tax collector, the village administrator, anyone she thought might be able to use the labor of her arms. The first to offer her something spread word of her abilities and of her diligence, but mainly of her willingness to go along with irregular pay, sometimes some stale cake and a piece of days-old fried fish, which Idalina received without protest or complaint. It was food which would hold off her son's hunger.

She insisted on keeping that child in school, even if only until the first exams. Even so, because she could barely earn enough to keep him fed, she knew that he would not be able to finish. She said so to the teacher, who got upset:

"But it would be a crime to take the little fellow out of school! Let him stay at my expense. I'll take care of whatever he needs."

"Thank you kindly, but don't put yourself out. Learning is not for the children of the poor. What is needed is to be able to read and write letters, and he's already learned enough to do that. And even if he hadn't, the only handout I'll accept is work."

"But you can't look at things that way! There's your son with that fine mind God gave him!"

"It would have been better if God had made him no smarter than an ass, because that seems to be what God created the poor to be. That is, if there is a God."

"What's that, woman! You..."

"That's how things look to me, ma'am, after all that's happened to me..."

Horrified, the teacher slammed the door on Idalina, who went to the priest's house to ask him to give her son work whitewashing and replacing tiles on the church.

On the day he was to begin, at sunrise, he went to where he would be working. Men and other boys were also there, smoking and talking, wraps over their shoulders. They all stood up and doffed their caps when they saw the priest walk up to the atrium with the foreman at his side and then stretch out his arm, point and call:

"You there, the little fellow!"

Joaquim came forward, eyes looking down, cap clutched in his nervous hands.

"Well, here's the new worker I told you about," said the priest to the foreman. "His mother, to tell you the truth, I haven't seen her much in church lately. It appears that she went so far as to say some pretty heretical things in the teacher's house. But we have to be forgiving. The boy's probably not good for much, he's so little. But, anyway, see if you can get him to do something to earn the money he'll get."

"Yes, sir, Father, we'll find something for him to do."

"All right. God keep you all. I have to go say Mass."

And the priest left.

The sacristan had tolled morning bells and was on his way down the bell tower wrapped up in his big red robe. Faces hidden in shawls and kerchiefs, two *beatas* went by, peering out of the corners of their eyes.

"Will you look who's there!" whispered one, elbowing the other.

"Idalina's little boy, the 'brain'! I'd heard his mother took him out of school."

"What else could she do!"

"And his father wanted him to have an education!"

"Vanity! Vanity!"

"Our Lord punishes and it's not with sticks and stones."

The foreman gave orders and everybody went to work.

Joaquim, along with Manuel Preseta, Inácio Choca, and João Gralha, was sent to the Canto das Canadas to dig from the cave. The foreman said to Manuel Preseta:

"You'll be in charge. Don't let them sit down on the job."

"Don't worry, boss," assured the man with the eyes of a hawk.

He slung a coil of rope over his shoulder, put some boxes of matches and pieces of tapers in his pocket. The others, two big husky fellows, carried burlap sacks. And all of them, the three of them and Joaquim bringing up the rear with his own load, set off on their way.

They went by the cemetery, reached the shore, jumped down, from rock to rock, and stopped at a kind of outcropping on top of a huge boulder. They dropped their loads on the ground, and Manuel Preseta, uncoiling the rope, said in a slow voice:

"Today, the school boy is going down into the cave to dig sand. This I've got to see." He was the father of one of Joaquim's school mates and at another time had been jealous of João Peixe-Rei's courage in slipping away. And—by a turn of the World—he had the son at his mercy. "Over here, my man." And he tied the rope under the boy's arms. "Off we go now!"

The face of the boulder was smooth, shiny, worn, with no place to get a grip, and went straight down to the rocks on which the sea washed up. Terrified, his eyes looking up, Joaquim wanted to speak, to shout, but the words stuck in his dry throat.

"Don't be afraid. The rope won't break," soothed Manuel Preseta. And to João Garralha: "Here, give me a hand letting the rope down."

And João Garralha and Inácio Choca broke into stupid, cruel laughter:

"What a mama's boy!"

His soul in agony and his eyes shut, Joaquim let himself hang from the rope and found himself at the bottom, stuck on a rock.

"No time to lose!" bellowed Preseta. "Untie the rope!"

And the rope went up, came back down with Inácio Choca, went up again, came down again, this time with the scraper and a pile of sacks.

"Hey, Inácio! Show the boy the right way to do things!" cackled Preseta.

"Yes, sir," promised Choca, undoing the pile of sacks. And to Joaquim:

"Get yourself into the cave."

Joaquim didn't move a muscle...

"In with you," insisted the other. "In there."

"In there!? How!?"

"Through those rocks. Get down on your belly and crawl."

"Get moving, boy!" guffawed Preseta on his perch.

"What a big shit-head!" rasped Garralha.

Joaquim got himself down and glimpsed an opening in the stone, a gap so narrow that it seemed not even a dog could get through. He stretched himself out, made himself long, became smaller than he really was, tore his tattered clothing, scraped his skin, scraped his muscles on the rough surface of the living rock, and went through the gap. On his belly, on his chest, on his legs, he felt the softness of the sand; in his eyes, he felt the blindness of the dark and over his whole body, much cold and humidity. It was hard for him to breathe, and his lungs hurt as if bursting. He tried to stand up. Something hit his head. A trickle of blood ran through his hair and warmed his face.

"I don't see anything," he shouted without mentioning his pain.

"Of course not!" Choca's voice was indifferent, as he stuck his own arm through the mouth of the cave. "Grab the scraper. When you've got it full, pass it out to me. First light the candle, cause you can't work in the dark."

Joaquim struck a match and a hole of light tore the darkness. He could see the sand cave—a roughly circular cavern, two to three meters in diameter and sixty to seventy centimeters high, crushed by the black carapace of the twisted rock, marked with deep crevasses and hanging points which were sharp as blades and continually dripping. If he tried to get up—new cuts would drip his body's blood.

And there he worked all day. He scraped sand, he filled up the scraper, pushed it out to Inácio Choca, who sent it back in to him after emptying it into the burlap sacks which Preseta and Garralha hoisted up on the rope. And again Joaquim filled the scraper and again he pushed it out to Inácio Choca.

At high tide, the sea lapped at his feet, at his legs, at his belly. With hollow, frightening sounds, it washed into the cracks and crevasses of the cave.

Outside, there was sun, sea, sky and the others talked about the weather and about the cornstalks drying up for lack of rain. Small farmers, they took work at the church to supplement their income when there was nothing to do in the fields.

"For the time being, there's nothing to be concerned about," pronounced Preseta. And in a good mood: "Inácio! Isn't that devil of a boy ever going to scrape up enough sand to fill that bag?"

Joaquim could only crawl around at work in the cave, only crawl around.

At sunset, when he got home, he couldn't stand up. His whole body ached. With water she had heated on the fire, his mother soaked his hands, his neck and swollen feet. With wet cloths, she washed the chafing spreading over his crotch and armpits. He complained:

"Those men are cruel."

"Cruel! What a silly thing to say!"

"They abuse me."

"They abuse you, come on! That's life. Life is hard. For the poor. You have to be patient."

"Well, if they weren't cruel, they wouldn't make me go into the cave!"

"And then what would you do?"

"There are so many things I could do!"

"Somebody has to get the sand."

"But does it always have to be me? No, those men are cruel. And the priest, too. The priest knows. And if he wanted to..."

"Don't ever talk like that, Joaquim!" His mother bit her lip to hold back her tears and stifle her sense of outrage. "Men are always good, they are our benefactors, they give us work so we can earn our daily bread. Let's pray."

Idalina hammered out words she no longer believed in.

The years went by. Joaquim met new labors, new struggles, new humiliations and kicks from fate and men. He dug other people's land under whips cracked by someone else. He went to sea, fishing: the others in the crew shoved him up to the bow oar—and if there was a squall, it was he who would get the first and heaviest slaps of the waves on his back; they set him to cutting up fish for bait (rotten fish many days old which would turn the stomach of the hardiest man) and Joaquim gritted his teeth and swallowed the first taste of bile so the others wouldn't have the satisfaction of seeing him get sick; if the tide seemed tricky and they couldn't drop anchor, or if, still along the coast, they were after baitfish they always left him with the oars, and if the rowing wasn't going right, he'd catch a smack on the head from the tiller handle or the bilge pump handle tossed by the master kneeling down, who followed that with thundering curses: "You dumb asshole! You stupid son of a bitch!"

Joaquim was becoming a man. Sometimes he felt like shouting: "Son of a bitch! Son of a bitch! You're the son of a bitch!" But he kept it to himself. He had heard the saying that a dog's bark is worse than his bite. And he would rather bite. Someday.

Much later, when the original organization of the whaling company changed, he managed a place to go whaling on Master Cabrita's boat. They rowed days and nights while hunting whales and towing the ones they'd harpooned back to land. And he was the last one to be given a rest by the officer. The palms he used to grip the oar bled, the seat of his pants wore through and his buttocks were raw from sitting so long on the bench in the boat.

"And that, my dear Francisco, is what I and this son of mine have gone through," concluded Idalina.

"Even now," grumbled Joaquim, who had heard everything his mother said without a word or gesture, "when we come in from whaling, that bastard of an officer and the others get to go home, sleep, screw around with their oversexed women..."

"My God, son! Hold your tongue!" interrupted his mother.

"...and I'm the one," contined the son, paying no mind to his mother's admonishment, "who has to stay at the dock and fire up the pots so they can boil down the blubber when they're finally gotten enough... And it goes badly for me if the pots aren't belching smoke when they get back! Afterward, they sent me into the whale's head to slop around in that crap. You know, I lost my father..."

A heavy silence hung over the kitchen; Francisco Marroco lit up a cigarette.

"I might be able to help you," he said.

"I wasn't talking so you'd feel sorry. Each one of us has a fate. I've never tried to avoid mine," replied Idalina.

"True! But from what I've seen and done in this World, I believe that handouts are insults, scorn thrown right at the poor. I am not rich and I didn't come here to insult anyone. I would like to help, just as João helped me. Does Joaquim know anything about keeping books?"

"Does he know anything about keeping books!? If it has to do with books, he knows about it. Even if he hadn't passed the first exam, he'd be the best around. Nobody can hold a candle to him. Even in the Winter he shuts himself up at home and whiles his time away reading books lent to him by the teacher, who never forgot him. Especially books that talk about ailments."

"And you, Joaquim, would you like to own a shop?"

The young man screwed up his eyes:

"Own a shop!?"

"Yes, have a business."

"And the money to buy?"

"That can be worked out."

"How?"

"I'll lend it."

"You'll lend it!?"

"Yes. It'll be an agreement, man to man."

"What's the interest?"

"I won't charge interest."

"You won't charge me interest!?"

"No."

"And if I couldn't pay you back?"

"You'll be able. And if you couldn't... Your father was

my best friend. But let's not talk about that right now. I'll have the money sent from America. I almost forgot: I have some souvenirs for you. And I want to be sure you'll come to my wedding."

"When's it going to be? You and Maria have had your eyes on each other since you were kids." And for the first time, Idalina smiled.

"It's set for two months from now, July 27."

(reunion)

Francisco Marroco walked along the old roads, among houses with their doors and windows open to the sea, houses surrounded by cornfields which were green in that year when there were good rains and favorable winds. He stopped to watch the men who, bent over, worked the land from dawn to dusk. They were free of the yoke of the boss who pays with his money, because a great part of the work was paid for with more work: help given to a neighbor was repaid with help from that neighbor. The most well-known the boys of our generation—left their blades where they tossed them in the middle of the field and came over to sit down on the wall next to the gate and chat a bit with Francisco Marroco:

"How're you getting along here?"

They took home-grown tobacco out of their pockets, but Francisco Marroco quickly held out a shiny pack of already-made cigarettes:

"Try one of these."

Cats went by, dogs went by, birds hidden away in the boughs of the myrtle trees and the incense trees cheeped, people out about their business went by with bundles of wood on their backs, the burro out in front, the cows behind. They, too, stopped to take a breather and exchange a few words. Time went by and at the last drag:

"Back to work," said the men in the fields, spitting on their palms.

Francisco Marroco kept on his rounds of visits to the places he remembered from his boyhood. He rediscovered the landscape as he remembered it and the people as he remembered them—and he rediscovered in them his own spirit of youth. The shadow of that chestnut tree, the vineyards at seaside, that deserted path, the black rocks of the coast... words of love he'd babbled out long ago, drops of sweat he'd shed, the confidence of João Peixe-Rei (the short visit of Captain Grilo and his ship)—and that completely tar-black night with its starts and fears... And inside of himself, Francisco Marroco discovered deep roots which came from his heart and linked him to all of that.

Thus daydreaming and wandering in a wide circle which would end up at Maria's house, packed with seamstresses and cooks, relatives and girl friends busy with preparations for the wedding, he passed through the Square at the edge of the port.

"Hey, Francisco! Hey, man!" called Master Cabrita, Master Basta and Master Calado, whaling officers who sat in the doorway to the boatshed on grounding poles and empty kegs and from morning to evening waited for the lookouts' skyrocket to burst. They were tough men, for it's only after experience that a man can take the helm of a boat. Master Basta no longer went out (but no one could separate him from his companions) and Cabrita, whom Joaquim had identified as his tormentor, was not long from retiring. Talking, smoking and dozing, they idled away the lazy hours of muggy weather and boredom, which were different and lively when the boats came from fishing for horse mackerel, or when the men who were working in the fields came back in the late afternoon. In the meantime, when they sensed someone on the road, they tried anxiously to make him stop, hoping for a few minutes of lively conversation:

"Hey, Francisco! What the hell kind of a hurry are you in!? Come on and sit a spell!"

Francisco Marroco leaned over the stern of the *Napoleão* or of the *Pátria*, the same boats with which Captain Silveira had started up the local whaling company, just like those in which he had risked his life so often when he was sailing on the *Queen of the Seas*. And he reminisced:

"Out in the Pacific, near New Caledonia... a whale off our bow..."

Off in the corners of the boatshed, over the belts and straps and around the wooden walls of the shed were piled tubs full of useless line, oars, drums, gaffs and broken masts, lances, harpoons and rusty spades.

Francisco Marroco didn't want to stay because he was in a hurry to be with Maria. But he kept on talking: about the death of his friend, terrible storms along Cape Horn, his arrival in America and trips across the country, days and days, nights and nights on the train, California...

Cabrita, Calado and Basta, who hadn't gone beyond the waters around the Island, listened to him, their mouths agape and their eyes wide with wonder:

"People around here..." Everything so small and difficult, they supposed their whale hunts paled in comparison to the other kind which took place far away on the great seas of the World.

Hours went by, the heat got worse, the morning sun rose in the cloudless sky. The conversation, which was becoming forced and monotonous, died away.

Francisco Marroco wanted to get away, but his legs seemed as heavy as hobbles and his eyelids drooped over his eyes. "Well now," he thought, making excuses to himself. "I'll wait around to buy some fish." And he asked:

"The boats?"

"They won't be long," yawned the others after a good while.

They arrived around noon. They beached on the pebbles, the fishermen jumped out and pulled them ashore, and unloaded the fish.

Francisco Marroco went up to Master Bendito, who was sorting his boat's fish and brusquely answering the women and boys who swarmed around him.

"Any fish for sale?"

"No, we didn't catch much and I need it for the fields. Take the parish's share."

Francisco Marroco waited, unsure, and lit a cigarette. The women grumbled, the boys squabbled, hanging around waiting for the tax collector to show up. And while they waited, the women Francisco Marroco knew best pestered him, all smiles and pleasant faces. The other ones, jealous of the honor of such informality, moved off to one side, staring annoyedly, because they saw and interpreted everything their own way. The boys were causing an uproar. Let their mothers turn up their noses: Did you ever see *anything* like him! It's disgusting! A Marroco! Let them turn their noses up as much as they wish, because for them, the young men, Francisco Marroco was a different kind of man. He had the guts to get away, to turn his back on the Island, and he was back, rich, from the fabulous paradise of fabulous America.

"Does the *americano* want something?" inquired Master Benedito obsequiously.

"I want some mackerel, but..."

"Why didn't you say something!?"

"I heard you..."

"*Obei,* man! For the *americano* there's always fish. We've even got a nice little swordfish there. It makes a very good soup."

"Your one-tenth?" asked the tax collector, with an eye on the mackerel stacked on the ramp.

"Right here, collector." And Benedito respectfully doffed his hat.

"The swordfish is supposed to go toward what we divide among ourselves, we already agreed," grumbled a fisherman.

"But the *americano* shouldn't have to pay for something we've caught! Come on!"

"*This much,*" announced the collector, beginning to auction off the one-tenth.

"*So much* more!"

And one after another, each fish from the one-tenth was sold off for whatever price the collector could get in the intense haggling.

"You guys string the fish so we can get going," Master Benedito told the men in his crew. Standing there, they waited for him to repeat the order. "Get with it! The piles are equal!" And to Francisco Marroco: "The *americano...*"

"Let's say half a dozen mackerel."

"And the swordfish?"

"No problem. And let's go have a drink."

Francisco Marroco went up to the shipyard with Master Benedito and his men, each one carrying his pole of fish in his hand. When they went by the boatshed:

"Let's go have a drink," he invited the three officers.

His jowls resting on his flabby chest, his fat hands folded on his big, lardy belly, all crumpled into his wicker chair in the back of his shop, next to the wine barrel, Master Augusto Bóia was dozing and snoring away. He half-opened his eyes, sensing a customer, and since that one was one more than none, he made the sacrifice of getting up and dragging himself to the counter. One more than none is what Francisco Marroco undoubtedly was, especially with all the others he had with him.

"Well, hello! How's the *americano* been getting on?" Master Augusto Bóia greeted them with half a dozen bows.

"Not too bad. I'd like to buy a round. What'll we have?" Francisco Marroco asked the fishermen and the three officers, who had their knives out and were cutting tobacco, some standing and others sitting on boxes which served as benches, lined against the wall in front of the counter.

Master Augusto Bóia patted the big wine jug and the bottle of cheap whiskey next to the plates on the wall rack. "Yes, sir! What'll it be?"

"A shot of whiskey for me," ordered Master Benedito.

"I'd rather have wine," preferred another.

"Me, too."

Fishermen from other crews came into the shop. And Francisco Marroco, not unmindful of his duty as an *americano:*

"Have a drink with me!"

The most hesitant, or most wily, politely declined, as they had been taught to do. They appreciated the invitation, but, no, sir, they weren't part of Master Benedito's crew. Even so, if they left without having had a drink, they'd say to everyone: "The big dunce! Can't even buy a round! Just because he's been to America... He can shove his money up his ass!" In that way they held Francisco Marroco, who did not want to be on the wrong side of his countrymen, up to public scorn:

"But it's my pleasure to pay! Oh, *yes!*" He paid them no mind.

"It would be an insult to the *americano!*" interrupted Bóia.

"An insult, *yes,*" agreed Francisco Marroco, grateful for the help.

"All right then, a glass of wine." And it was as if they were doing him a big favor.

"Whiskey for me."

And wine and whiskey flowed from the big jug and the bottles into the glasses, while Bóia wiped the drops from the top of the counter with a rag.

Francisco Marroco offered cigarettes, smoked, and also had his glass filled. The fishermen stayed around, enjoying the pleasure of the cool shade. They looked quietly at the full glasses, enjoyed smoking those good cigarettes. And they spoke: "The land of America, the sea..." Recently, they couldn't stop talking about the Our Lady of Life Bank, which had been founded on Faial a short time before.

Field representatives, appointed in the towns and in some of the villages of the four islands in the district, went along the roads and pathways, banging on every door, pressuring everyone they found. With some, they appealed to the sense of local chauvinism. With others, they appealed to the ambition for easy wealth. With still others, they pushed the need for protection against some future calamity. People could be sure, or so they argued, that no one would lose his money if he deposited it in the Our Lady of Life Bank. And no one should be embarrassed or worried because he didn't have a large amount on hand. Well, ten *mil-réis* coins stuck away in the corner of a drawer would always be ten *mil-réis*, while in the Bank, ten *mil-réis* now and ten *mil-réis* a few months from now would add up to a nice tidy sum, which, later, with interest, could be an amount of great possibilities. A setback, an illness... And he'd be contributing to the prosperity of the Islands and their people, because the men who founded the Bank wanted nothing for themselves.

The seed of those words did not fall on barren ground. And while few had ten *mil-réis* to spare, everyone was dazzled with the idea, setting about making calculations and plans. An ox they might sell, a share from whaling... But uncertain, because money takes an arm and a leg to come by, they had gone to see Master Augusto Bóia, their long-time advisor on all sorts of matters.

Concerning the Bank, however, Bóia had grunted: "Huh? Well! Yes, sir, what can I say?" He really felt like fighting the Our Lady of Life Bank to the death because it had not appointed a representative in the village, and he was available. All he had to do was open his mouth, and for miles around, there wouldn't be a soul who wouldn't accept and do what he suggested. Nevertheless, that wasn't the answer. He was nobody's fool. He sensed the claw of important and self-interested commercial and political forces behind the whole matter, and if a man ought always to be at peace with God, he should also never get in bed with the Devil.

Deprived of Master Augusto Bóia, who listened to them close-mouthed on the other side of the counter, they sounded out Francisco Marroco:

"You, you've travelled out there in the wide world..."

"From here to there... Now, here..."

Francisco Marroco disappointed them with his hesitations.

"Drink up and forget about that nonsense," said Master Benedito, making himself appear knowledgeable. "Who is there on these dark stones who can save money to put in the Bank? That wouldn't even cross a fool's mind! Over in America..."

"Over that way..." Current rumors were discussed: people from Piedade and Prainha selling lands for money to put in the Bank. "The interest... And then there's no rain, no wind."

"As far as I'm concerned, it would never be my father's son. Now, those who might have money off to the windward, like Mr. Francisco, who's come from *Calafona*...'"

And Master Benedito and his companions were curious to see what might be coming from Francisco Marroco, who, pretending he didn't know what going on, was telling more stories about America and the *Queen of the Seas*. Sometimes about the strange, exotic women he'd known in faraway ports of Africa, Asia, the Pacific, New Caledonia.

The fishermen listened wide-eyed and downed their drinks quickly, putting out the fire which was burning them up inside.

"Let's go home." Master Benedito got up.

"Master, you didn't give me the price for the mackerel." And Francisco Marroco took out his wallet.

"No need to talk about that!"

"No need!?"

"No, sir, no need!"

"But I want to pay!"

"Oh, boy. Man, don't insult me! Take the mackerel, and when you need more... No problem! Master Benedito'll be around!"

The men downed the last drinks and set off for home.

"I've got to get going, too," and Francisco Marroco got up.

Master Augusto Bóia, however, insisted on the honor of a conversation between the two of them alone, even if for just a few minutes:

"Well, now, the *americano*... Yes, sir, you got yourself some nice little mackerel. They're good with garlic juice and hot peppers. That Benedito! A real bower and scraper. Me, I can't eat spicy foods any more. I really used to like them, but my stomach won't let me." He let loose a deep belch and rubbed his belly with a fat hand: "You'll have to excuse me! It's because of what ails me, and I who used to be so healthy. I had to give up everything! Yes, sir, everything! I was a whaling officer and I no longer go out. That bum, Calado, goes in my place. He used to be my harpooner. A clod! Me, well, besides never having left this place, and it's not to toot my own horn, 'cause that's not the sort of person I am, but the truth is, let it be said, that I always pulled my weight. I caught many whales, yes sir, I never owed my share to someone else's efforts. And as for sailing! I myself was born to be a ship's captain. Now, I'm good for nothing. I'm in the management of the whaling company because I'm a member, I have a few shares which my father, God rest him, left me. But that! A lot of work! Some day I'll get rid of everything and keep just the shop, which gives me enough to scratch myself with." Master Augusto Bóia pointed around vaguely and lazily at calicoes, denims, linens, cottons, flannels, boxes and bottles with attractive labels which filled the shelves, sacks of flour and sugar, cans of oil and crates of soap stacked underneath. "That's it, yes, sir. I'll just keep the shop. I feel old. Of course, you know, get rid of my shares in the company, I won't do that." And as if a sudden idea came to him: "And the *americano* must also become a member! Something from our ancestors..."

And Francisco Marroco, standing in the doorway:
"See you later. I left the fish in the sun."
"That's right. You'd better be going!" And Master Augusto Bóia stood there thinking: "This devil must have money! He pretended he didn't hear..."

Cabrita, Basta and Calado were dozing at the door of the boatshed. Master Benedito, his crew and the others, who had been drinking with them, were already long gone.

They were speculating, slowly travelling the bad roads toward the Sun's fire.

"A straightforward man, this Marroco."
"Seems so."
"And he must have money!"
"Most likely."
And Master Benedito, in front of his house:
"Here's where I stop. We going to sea tomorrow?"

"If the Master feels like it..."

"Well, then, see you tomorrow. Bring potatoes for bait." And he pushed on the gate.

Sure that they wouldn't be heard, the others whispered among themselves:

"That son of a bitch! There's never an *americano* he doesn't get his hands on."

"Mind your own business."

"What about self-respect?"

At the kitchen door, her body straight and her hands on her hips, Rita Benedita waited for her husband, who was coming with two mackerel in hand:

"That's all you got with you?"

"Yes."

"You didn't catch any more than that?"

"We did."

"And you went and sold it!? Don't you know we have people coming to turn the fields next week?"

"I didn't sell it. I gave it away."

"You gave the fish away!? How about this man here!..."

"I gave it to young Marroco, the *americano*."

"Ah! So that's it!" Rita Benedita's full-moon face relaxed.

"I bet he's got some money stashed away."

"If anyone does, he's the one."

"If he could stake me to a pair of overalls and enough to buy me a new net... with what we got last year I'd thought to buy the boat."

"Well, latch on to the guy, 'cause he's probably got more than enough."

(cans, guitars, songs and party-
ing on the wedding night)

A happening like Francisco Marroco's wedding to Roque's Maria had never been seen. And from then on nobody doubted that he had more than enough.

Since the whole village was invited, the number of onlookers was so large that many couldn't fit into the church. Among those present were Idalina and her son, both very well-dressed because that was what Francisco Marroco had insisted on. The two had places of honor near the bride and groom at the large table at the wedding banquet. Three fat oxen were slaughtered and the guests stuffed themselves, as did all the people in the surrounding countryside because Francisco Marroco had his plenty shared with them since they could not share the happiness which filled his heart.

That night, in the light of the moon and the acetylene lamps, a huge party was held. Can beaters came, as was the custom, to bang out their best wishes to the newlyweds. They ate, drank and took part in the dancing. And everybody sang and everybody danced, except for Idalina and her son, despite Francisco Marroco's encouragements as he passed by them.

"This is not a day to be sad! A happy face and an open heart!" And just between themselves: "I haven't forgotten what we talked about."

And he and Maria, now husband and wife, whirled around in the turns of the *chamarrita*.

"Do you remember?" she whispered, almost beside herself with happiness. And the two of them, looking into each other's eyes, holding each other's hands, each's body close to the other's, remembered that summer's night during a certain long-ago grape harvest. They both remembered—and so did Francisco Marroco's mother and father.

The old man could no longer hold in the joy that was bursting inside him. He went into the house, took the guitar down from its nail in the corner next to the clock, shook the dust and cobwebs off, had someone go buy brand-new strings and, since he had been reborn, there he resurrected the old guitar, which had seemed dead since the night his son had slipped away. With both his eyes shining, he vigorously strummed out the *chamarrita:* new *chamarrita,* old *chamarrita,* high *chamarrita,* low *chamarrita,* and the middle *chamarrita* and the sad one! And up he stands, grabs his wife, the two of them bounce onto the dance floor and he making the calls while playing the guitar: "Dance! Jump forward! Close the circle! Dance again! This lady! No, I don't want this one! Away with you! Dance once more! Open the keep!" And so he called to the rhythm of the music and his sweet lady too was dancing and singing fine old tunes, she who when young didn't dance or sing, that is to say, ever.

What it was was that their son had come from America and was married that night!

ON THE ISLAND FOREVER

(the americano's money)

Francisco Marroco decided to stay on the Island forever. Maria asked him to—and what had she ever asked of him that he didn't do? His parents asked him to in the quiet, silent language of their faces. But, even if no one had asked him, Francisco could never again cut himself loose from the Island.

That morning while they were having breakfast, he talked about his plans: he wanted to repair the house—new doors, windows, floor and roof—and add on two or three rooms. And he wanted to buy land enough for his family.

Maria and his parents listened to him happily. The daughter of a farmer, Maria loved the earth: she loved to smell its strong odor when the plow turned it, to gather the harvest after, and throughout the year to knead and bake the bread which came from it. As for his mother—it was enough to have her son before her eyes and right up close to her heart until death should carry her off. His father was the one who, having spent his life on the dark stones of Pico, thought it his duty to give some advice: his son should buy land, but not sink all his money in it. In a year of drought or cyclones, only money could save him from hunger. And he shouldn't be hasty: since the people were all fired up with the news about the Bank, there were sure to be some who'd want to sell land. But when it was all sorted out, and since many small lots were not worth much, for a man to have a piece here and a chunk there only meant a hellish life along those mean roads and pathways. It would be good to have everything in one tract or at least in two or three enclosures not far from each other. In Figueirinha, Almeida's enclosure had been up for sale for months. A large, deep enclosure, it was enough to yield more than two hundred and forty bushels of corn.

"What're they asking for it?" Francisco Marroco was interested.

"I heard talk about three hundred and fifty mil-réis."

"More or less three hundred and fifty dollars."

"Someone who offers three hundred, maybe less... And if two or three other pieces came up near it..." And without transition, the old man spoke about repairs to the house. "Whatever you do will be for you. Your mother and I are no longer important."

And everyone saw masons and carpenters knocking down walls and wood to make the small old house big, new and pretty. Everybody saw—and everybody heard: Francisco Marroco had given money as down payment to Almeida to buy the Figueirinha land. And from that, one could deduce how serious he was about his decision.

"How can a man who's been all over the world settle in this out-of-the-way place?" wondered the youngest.

"What he's got is a lot of *monin,*" envied the most ambitious.

And because of the lot of money, there was many a man who went out of his way to fall into the good graces of Francisco Marroco.

The priest with his obsequious movements and oily voice had already been to call on him.

"Today's the first chance I've had to stop by. Parish affairs keep me very busy..." After a long and insignificant conversation: "Our little church is in bad need of a few repairs. The spray from the sea nearby... I thought about writing to America to some of our former parishioners who're over there and I remembered that Mr. Francisco Marroco could give me some addresses. I'm also counting on your generosity and would be honored if you'd chair the committee which will be in charge of the repairs."

The officers of the Holy Ghost brotherhoods came, too:

"The year-end festivals in decline... The old people's things that we can't let die: promises made when the earth shook, when the fire burst forth from the volcanoes, and in the years when there were droughts and cyclones."

And stuffed into the tightness and the formality of their Sunday suits, the three members of the Village Council also knocked at his door:

"New elections! There will be new elections," began the president.

And the other two:

"Yes, sir, new elections, a few months from now."

The president:

"If the *americano* should wish to be part of our party's slate... The opposition is saying... that this time they'll bring us down!"

The others:

"And it would be a disaster for our land if such a thing should happen."

The president:

"With you up for president, we'd win for sure!"

They kept insisting. Francisco Marroco, however, would not let himself be convinced.

Finally, a well-spoken, well-dressed individual in a necktie came around:

"You are Mr. Francisco Marroco who arrived not too long ago from America?"

"Yes, I am."

"A pleasure to meet you, I've come on behalf of the Our Lady of Life Bank; I have the honor to be its representative and I wish only to be of service to you."

"Uh-huh!"

"They sent me specifically to..." And the man spoke about the generous goals of the Our Lady of Life Bank and about the independent character of the men running it, about its solid financial condition, with reserve funds already deposited in the most well-known national and foreign banks, about the high rates of interest the bank could offer...

Yes, Francisco Marroco had already heard. In truth, he had managed to save a little money in America, but... And cautiously:

"I still haven't decided if I'll leave it there. Not that it's a large amount..."

"And how much do the American banks pay you?"

"Five percent."

"You see? We pay nine percent! Almost twice as much! No one pays more!"

"That's good! Well, what about security?"

"Security!? There's no bank more secure than ours! But don't take just my word! Listen to other people. Your school's teacher keeps her savings in it. Get the facts. Then, come talk!"

The representative had come in the *Varina,* the launch which in those days connected Faial and Pico, calling at ports around the Island with freight and passenger service. All the people, who would stand on the pier, in the square and on the atrium to enjoy the day the boat would come, saw him get off and head for Francisco Marroco's house, and at dusk, when he came to Master Augusto Bóia's shop for half a kilo of sugar, everybody who was there tried to get him to satisfy their curiosity:

"So, the Bank's representative stopped by your house, did he!?"

At that moment, the teacher, a middle-aged man who'd succeeded the woman who had the job before she retired, came in. Keeping intact his belief in the merit and nobility of his mission, it was only to buy cigarettes that he set foot in Master Augusto Bóia's shop, which he considered a vulgar, coarse tavern like all taverns. Nevertheless, when he did come in he'd stay for a while, standing against the counter for a smoke, so that his student's fathers wouldn't put him down as snobbish because he wouldn't associate with them. And he practiced what he said was the broadening of his action beyond the unwhitewashed four walls of his ramshackle schoolhouse.

That day, Francisco Marroco remembered a ploy. He bought wine or whiskey for those who wanted it and turned to the teacher:

"Will you have something?"

No, he wouldn't, thank you very much anyway, but he didn't touch alcoholic beverages.

"Some Port, Madeira wine, a liqueur," insisted Francisco Marroco.

"Please forgive me, but I can't drink, my doctor won't let me," the teacher explained. And to the others: "Don't mind me."

With their glasses full, those present again wanted to know what Francisco Marroco, who without revealing what he thought, was trying to get the teacher to say about the question of there being branches of other banks on Faial. Not that the Our Lady of Life Bank wasn't a good thing! Interest, good rate. So good that a body would stand in line for it. Not even in America was it as high!

He took the bait, the teacher: they should excuse him, but let him explain. And to Francisco Marroco:

"What do you think? The Our Lady of Life Bank is the most formidable economic revolution ever seen on these islands! Thanks to it and to the men who founded and unselfishly direct it, we will progress in the next ten years more than we have progressed in the last four centuries we've been here! Do you see those roads? To live on an island, it's clear to see, is to live on a chain. On ours, from the town to here on the south side and from Prainha de Cima on the north side, no one dares travel by land, no matter where they have to go, unless it's absolutely necessary, because the roads are so frightful they terrify us. We have the sea. But if the sea is rough... How many people have died because we couldn't get them to a doctor in time? And what about the water supply? Where are the fountains to bring it to the communities? Thank God it has rained these last few years. But when the drought and cyclones come..."

"We die out here like dogs." And the men somberly wrapped themselves in the smoke from their cigarettes.

"Well," affirmed the teacher, "the Our Lady of Life Bank proposes changing all that! Roads to connect village to village; roads going inland so we can get more use of our fields from coast to mountain; a water system on this and on all the other islands. And the wealth of the sea? The fish we don't go after because we don't have large, well-equipped boats, nor processing plants to make use of them? And our whaling industry which needs to be torn out of the primitive state in which it flounders? And with the Our Lady of Life Bank—everything will be transformed! In a short while, we shall see a new life arise! And our people will live happily, and we will never have to wander the World suffering, as did Mr.

Francisco Marroco, to get away from hunger and poverty. Just yesterday, I read an article in the *Island Democrat*. It was saying that the Our Lady of Life Bank is *our* Bank! Whoever has money, a lot or a little, it doesn't matter how much, it's his patriotic and local duty to put it in the service of *our* Bank! Besides, no other bank gives better guarantees!'' concluded the teacher.

Late at night, when everyone had gone to bed, Francisco Marroco heard someone knock at his door. When he opened it, there, with a lantern in one hand and the waist of his trousers in the other, was Master Augusto Bóia.
"Why, Master Augusto!"
"Good evening."
"Good evening! Come in."
"Just a few words in private." And Bóia looked around, from one side to the other, like someone afraid the dark night might have eyes to see and ears to hear with. "Over in the shop there're always people coming in..."
"Well then, come in, come in. We'll have to use the kitchen because the rest of the house with the men working... Sit down, sit down here."
"Thank you. My friend, you'll have to excuse me." And Bóia, folded over the bench Francisco Marroco had indicated, rubbed his jowls as if looking in his soft fat for the right words to use in a delicate situation. "The best thing," he decided, "is to get right to the point. The management of the whaling company had a meeting today, and your name, my friend, was mentioned many times."
Francisco Marroco tucked a cigarette into the corner of his mouth. Bóia went on:
"Yes, sir. If you wanted... What my associates on management wanted me to tell you... They were all going to come, but I said it wasn't necessary, that we were friends, and

well, they... It could've waited until tomorrow, there's no hurry, but I was passing by. Well, anyway, uh, if you felt like it, it'd be no problem for you to buy a few shares..."

Francisco Marroco leaned forward, lighting his cigarette from the lantern:

"You know, don't you, that I didn't come back from America a millionaire!"

Bóia watched in the expression of the other for the effect of his words:

"But neither is anybody asking you to blow it all."

"And how much does a share earn?" asked Francisco Marroco without really caring to know.

"Well, sir! For anyone with money to spare, there's no better way to put it to use, you can take my word for it. Now, about how much a share earns... If many whales are caught and the oil gets a good price, sometimes you get the money you put in back in a year."

"That's a hundred percent!" marvelled Francisco Marroco.

"It's not always the way it turns out; let's not say that things are one way and have them turn out another way!"

"Even so. Many people could still get rich. Are there many shareholders?"

"Well, no! Many shareholders, yes, sir, but, except for myself and two or three others, and yourself, if you go along with us, the rest of them don't matter. In the old days... But mostly after Captain Silvestre died..."

After Captain Silvestre died—and that was something Bóia didn't get into—the conditions of life in the whaling company changed quite a bit. Several operations were started in nearby ports—Ribeiras, Lages, Santo Amaro, São João—and one in the village itself. At sea, hemmed in by the boats of rivals, the boats from Calheta either cowardly let the others take the whales, spouting, away from their bows, or they went after them and put up a fierce fight, taking chances with risky maneuvers in which the least danger would be a smashed boat, but many times things would wind up with a man permanently crippled or dead. But even with an endless number of dangers to add to so many other unavoidable ones in that kind of work, the real whaler preferred to take the chance.

On Faial, after the death of old Crown and later his son, the grandson, John Crown, had taken charge of the business and there, in the old office, the squabbling between the representatives of the various Pico operations went on, with each one indifferent to shrinking prices, trying to sell the oil produced before the others could. So profits got smaller, without any lessening of expenses.

Beyond that, other founding partners had died. Their shares, divided and subdivided in a tapestry of inheritances, were no longer worth much at all. And it happened that many of those heirs were women, and that meant that the number of strong-minded shareholders who were at the same time whalers decreased, while the number of whalers who, with no share in the boats they crewed, received only a salary, which was more and more of a pittance, increased.

Finally, shortly before the return of Francisco Marroco, the first motorized launches were bought in Lages and Ribeiras. By then, the operations in São João and Santo Amaro had been dissolved, and, in the village, only the original one was still in business. Its boats, however, were falling apart—ribs showing, sides crumbling, water seeping in through the uncaulked areas, sails tearing at the slightest breeze, oars and masts rotting to pieces. Because they had no launch, when they did go out, the men got there late and found only dead whales belonging to other whalers, or whales frightened by those who'd arrived earlier, which wouldn't let anyone get close. There was just enough money made to scatter crumbs among whalers and partners after the unavoidable necessities had been taken care of.

Master Augusto Bóia knew about this situation better than anyone else, although he wasn't the only one to be acquainted with the full gravity of it. He feared its consequences and saw in Francisco Marroco's money a life line. Nevertheless, he fumbled with weak, timid half-words which said nothing:

"In Captain Silvestre's time, you already know... But, even today..."

"What I don't understand," and Francisco Marroco lit another cigarette, "is why you and the other more important shareholders don't apply your money to buy more shares instead of bringing me into such a mess."

"Well, sir, we're getting old. I'm almost sixty-five. The others are my age or older. When we die, all of us with cartloads of heirs, the company will be left without any shareholder with enough in it to make things worth the trouble. And without the whaling company, and there's nothing else in the village to produce even a penny's worth, what kind of future will there be for our children?" So, if you could..."

"His mouth is watering," thought Francisco Marroco. And he mentally counted the hours the clock struck in the inner room: ten... eleven... twelve... Midnight! Midnight already!

"Do you want my answer today?" he yawned.

"No, no. There's no hurry!" And Master Bóia got up.

"So, tomorrow or the day after..."

"Yes, sir! And a good night! Good night and sorry to have bothered you."

"No bother. Good night."

"Good night!"

And with the door closed, Francisco Marroco grumbled: "What a pain!"

In the warmth of the inner room, where the two couples—his father and mother, himself and Maria—were temporarily sleeping, making do because of the repairs to the house, father and son had a long conversation. The next day, Francisco Marroco went to see Bóia in his shop:
"I accept your invitation to be a shareholder in the company."
"How much are you putting in?"
"Two hundred mil-réis. As soon as the money comes from America."
"Yes, sir!"
It was good amount, so good that Francisco Marroco became one of the largest shareholders in the old operation. It was not, however, enough to take care of the many serious problems the company had.
"That's grand, yes, sir, and thank you, thank you very much!" And Master Augusto Bóia smiled, certain that his wiles would pry something more from Francisco Marroco's pockets.

(ambitions, resentments, hatreds,
cloistered
on the dark stones of
the island)

The enthusiastic euphoria over the Our Lady of Life Bank continued spreading to all corners of the Island.

Many heads of family wound up scratching together whatever they could lay their hands on and, in a final expression of anguished hope, turned it over to the Our Lady of Life Bank for safekeeping: dollars sent by relatives in America, money diverted from the hunger of many mouths and the nakedness of many bodies and painfully gathered in hopes of building a house, buying a piece of land or a patch of grapevine. And many would do the same when someone wanted to buy their little bits of land—rockbeds (as they called them) from which they could never squeeze a thing worth their hard work—hoping that way to gain some little profit from the sale, a return of nine percent, which was a yield greater than that of all the corn, potatoes or wine they could produce.

In the village, among those whose assets allowed them to join up, the most cautious still hesitated and hung around Francisco Marroco, hoping for a word or gesture—after all, he was a man who'd seen the world. Francisco Marroco was cautious in both word and deed, afraid people might blame him later if some unforeseen disaster should take place. "One can never be too careful," it was said. "Let everyone do what he thinks best." Nevertheless, he too looked for advice from whoever might speak with authority. He had heard the teacher—and on his occasional trips into the town, he went to the town treasurer, to the town administrator, to the businessmen of the Casa Santíssima—all of them enlightened people who repeated, with different words, the same thing the schoolmaster had told them.

He wound up writing to America, having them send the money he'd left there and, when the letter in answer came, he took the *Varina* to Faial, got off at the Santa Cruz pier and went straight to the Our Lady of Life Bank. The director received him in his luxurious office, with an overabundance of friendliness and kind words.

"By entrusting your capital to us, you are contributing to the prosperity of our beloved land!"

As the only businessman in the village, Master Augusto Bóia was also the local postmaster. Francisco Marroco's letters passed through his hands—and, when he saw him board the boat for Faial, he knew what was happening and what he was going to do. Hiding his intentions, he passed on what he knew to the people who hung around his shop, and they immediately tossed it to the four winds of local gossip. Those who were waiting for a signal from him no longer had any reason to doubt the Our Lady of Life Bank. And all those who had to sell something to raise capital began to knock on his door mysteriously and secretively.

Francisco Marroco could have bought all the lands in the village and the whole whaling company, except for Master Augusto Bóia's part. He limited himself to the lot at Figueirinha, promised to him by Almeida, and two or three other pieces nearby, as his father had advised, and to investing the promised two hundred *mil-reis* in the whaling company.

He answered the requests of the priest and the majordomos of the Pentecost festivals—and turned down all invitations to assume positions of power and prestige. "I wasn't born for that" was his excuse.

He lovingly took charge of the work on the additions to the house, and with the pride of a new owner, he toured the lands he'd bought, planning here the construction of a wall, there the cutting of a myrtle, in another place the widening of a doorway. He came home at night beaming. His eyes would look into Maria's and look down at her swollen belly—and his heart was moved at the thought of the life growing in that belly.

As the weeks went by, he made fewer visits to the shop of Master Augusto Bóia, who understood it was in his best interest to be nice to the *americano* to get him to put more capital into the whaling company.

Francisco Marroco went back to Faial two or three more times, the last one with Idalina's Joaquim. This coming and going intrigued everyone, especially Master Augusto Bóia, who felt betrayed, despite the insistent press of his old shrewdness, because Francisco Marroco did not confide the reason for those trips in him. "The devil take the man who knows how to be patient!"

The mystery cleared up on the day when the *Varina* arrived and unloaded merchandise not for Master Augusto Bóia.

It was an unexpected surprise, when Idalina's Joaquim appeared on the pier, Francisco Marroco protecting him with his authority, and ordered the cargo sent to Malhinha's house, where there were shelves and the counter from an old establishment which had been closed up for a long time. They were all shocked:

"Idalina's Joaquim with a shop! Well, what do you know!"

"And Francisco Marroco helping that stinker!"

"The world's coming to an end!"

And they went on their way, faces turned contemptuously away. The busy bee of curiosity was not to be stopped, however. And soon everyone stopped by to peek at the inside of the new establishment—the men with their hands in their pockets, cigarettes tucked in their silent lips, the women, mouths pursed, looking askance from under the shawls tied around their heads. They were a little disappointed because the quality and arrangement of everything seemed like that of what was piled up in Bóia's shop. The only difference was Joaquim himself, his body still skinny and dressed in rags, leaning on the counter, his eyes buried in a book—the greasy medical tome which he had inherited from the recently deceased schoolmistress. Beyond that, the only difference, on the other side of the counter, were the three pine tables with benches around them and decks of cards on top—Francisco Marroco's idea.

On windy and rainy days, which made work in the fields and fishing at sea impossible, Joaquim would raise his eyes in an unsure invitation:

"Come in out of the weather. Pretty bad out there! If you like..." And he pointed awkwardly at the pine tables and the decks of cards waiting for players.

Loosening up little by little, the men began to sit down and get interested in the pastime, wanting today to free themselves from yesterday's bother, tomorrow wanting to repeat the pleasure of the previous day's winning hand. It wasn't real gambling because no one bet money.

In the midst of the hands being played came the tobacco, the swig of whiskey, the glass of wine. And Joaquim never got to night time with an empty cash drawer.

In their homes, the men commented:

"What the hell, the boy's got everything. You can buy almost anything there." And if the women didn't think it was right to leave Bóia, who'd been selling them what they needed for many years, often on credit: "If he didn't sell, he wouldn't make any money. The other one's prices aren't any higher. And he needs to live, too."

And in the shop of Idalina's Joaquim, customers appeared not just for the cards and smokes, the wine and the whiskey, even though he had not yet learned how to smile as a rule and how to make people feel welcome. One day, Francisco Marroco, who happened to be there, saw him look with hatred at some of those who'd harassed him when he was a child. And he suggested:

"Look, Joaquim, it's all water over the dam. What's done is done. And keep in mind what I'm saying. If you're going to run a business, you can't hold grudges against people. A paying customer is always a good customer. And a good customer, no matter who, is always a good person. I'm not a businessman, but it seems to me that's the way things have to work. But you're a man, and I have nothing to do with your life. What is true, though, what is true is that I was your father's friend!"

The advice took hold. At least Francisco Marroco supposed it did. And in the presence of his contentment and the mother's joy, the young man was taking his first steps on the road to prosperity.

Master Augusto Bóia was the one who was not happy with Joaquim's prosperity. No one was more astounded than he when he saw the unloading of merchandise not addressed to him. For a long time, his had been the only establishment and it was an insult, an outrage, what they were doing to him. He hated Idalina's Joaquim, he hated Francisco Marroco. His skin crawled when he remembered that he, Augusto Bóia, he brought the *americano—americano!*—into the whaling company and, without managing to pry from him the expected amount of money, he saw himself now obliged to have him as a partner. A partner! Yes, sir! A partner! It was understandable that someone else might have been taken in, but that it should have been he! He, the man called Augusto Bóia! Still, he kept his resentment to himself and put on friendly airs with all who came to trade with him, especially with Francisco Marroco. The worst of it was that his customers were deserting him. The decks of cards he'd tossed out on the tables in imitation of the other's come-on didn't do him any good. The days added up to weeks and months. His best customer took the long way around, and Master Augusto Bóia's sales were rare—sometimes not even a paltry glass of whiskey. He slept badly, ate worse, let life pass him by as he sat disinterestedly in his wicker chair. His thoughts grew muddled, he planned terrible vengeance to feed the hatred he could barely hide.

"I'll smash the ugly face of that stupid son of Idalina's!" he thought, his eyes wide open in the silence of his deserted shop. "That bum can't even show gratitude for everything I sold his mother on credit when his father skipped off!" And with his thoughts overflowing with bitterness, the punishment of a punch seemed inconsequential. He'd finish him off. One of those Winter nights with a driving rain, heavy winds and tar-black darkness in which no one dares set foot out, he'd knock on his door, call him out and—wham!—a bash on his head and that'd be it. He had an iron bar lying around! Then a few steps more and he'd send the *americano* to hell, too. Anyone who could've seen the expression on his face as he raised his trembling arms up in a gesture of vengeance, only to let them fall, limp and powerless, would have been horrified. "In my day!" And a tear rolled down his face. If that kind of night came around, nowadays, he wouldn't live through the fever which still bothered him. And he had no illusions: he was no longer the man for such a risky act.

But he still had his voice! Bóia's face and eyes lit up. What he had to do was to put words to work: to let loose one of those rumors which unsettled the best of reputations, to ruin Joaquim and Marroco and force them to close the door of that dump because of the outrage of upright people who'd be scandalized at the shameful stories going around. And as soon as his last, faithful customers showed up, the ones who came by for a drop now and then:

"It's true! Didn't you hear?..." he began confidentially.

No, they hadn't. And what should they have heard? They looked at each other in surprise because Bóia had never shared any information with them.

"What they're saying about the *americano,* about the younger Marroco..."

"Perhaps his money isn't what they say," sniffed the drinkers.

"That's not it! But drink up, 'cause today I'm buying. Well, it's everywhere."

"What's everywhere?" And the man who asked the question downed the glass on top of the counter while the

others wondered: "What the hell does this guy want?"
"The *americano* and Idalina..." he whispered.
"The *americano* and Idalina?"
"Yes, Joaquim's mother, João Peixe-Rei's widow. You really don't know!? Well, then..." And Bóia told them the story he made up.
The others smoked, drank and listened.
"And the fact is that before the bum shipped out, he was getting some on the sly, poor João Peixe-Rei," concluded Bóia.
"Before shipping out!? But he wasn't more than fifteen! Sixteen at most!"
"Yes, sir! That's the way it was. And it was to keep everyone else and the son, who caught them, quiet... well, anyway, he took them under his wing."
The others laughed:
"Idalina, what's she got? Just skin and bones! Marroco'd better hope he can handle the woman he's got at home; she's a cow in need of a real bull!"
They finished their drinking, went off and told everybody and they laughed—for the first time a derisive laugh at Master Augusto Bóia.

(above all—a man dreams)

In the finally finished house, halfway up the slope, dominating the land and the sea with its white walls trimmed in black, its green doors and its red roof covered with tiles from Marseilles, the first child of Francisco Marroco and Maria was born.
Spring was moist and calm, and when Francisco Marroco would come home, happy that his corn was looking fine, he'd run happily to Maria and ask excitedly, hoping nothing had happened while he was away:

"Our little boy? Our António?" They had named him António after his father and Tony of the *Queen of the Seas*. "Our little boy is sleeping. He's just finished nursing. Let him be or you'll wake him up." And Maria pointed to the cradle.

And he didn't touch, didn't stir the child; he was even afraid he'd hurt his little boy with his clumsy hands. Standing still, shaking with tenderness, he looked at that beloved little body: his flesh's flesh and Maria's flesh! Blood of his blood and Maria's blood! His heart's heart and Maria's heart! The union of the two of them in one person just through the miracle of love.

And he dreamed. He would do everything to give his son the nice, easy life he never had! And he was afraid of life—because of his son!

His son! No! There, next to his son, he was not going to worry about the terrible lies which Master Augusto Bóia's hatred was vomiting!

Francisco Marroco wasn't worried, nor was Idalina's Joaquim, whose belly was getting fat and flabby, who had money in his cash drawer and prestige in the village, thanks to his credits as a good businessman—and to his reputation as someone who *understood things*.

That's what they began to think of him when he began to give sound advice about home remedies and ointments for all sorts of ailments. Happy because they had someone around who *understood things* and kept them from dying like dogs. At the slightest shiver or suspicion of pain, they'd go looking for him immediately or call him to their bedside. They trusted his understanding so much that they were loath to go to the doctor—a difficult step in any case—before he advised them to, not because of... incompetence in the doctor, but only to make sure Joaquim had his say. Something no one dared to do was to have the doctor's prescription filled without showing it to Joaquim and getting his approval. Why, he knew more than all the doctors in the World!

His reputation spread and, from far off, the disillusioned sick came seeking the miracle of his cures. In the shop, people began to see pharmaceutical packages, wrapped up, on the shelves and on the counter, along with bolts of fabric, bottles of whiskey and jugs of wine. And after seeing, feeling and listening, Joaquim prescribed and sold pills, syrups, powders—and injections, which he stuck in the arms of those who wanted them. And he pulled teeth, set banged-up legs and feet, treated anxieties, boils and carbuncles. He also sold other sorts of things from his shop and he prospered, although he continued wearing rags, gave no indication of a wish to take a woman in marriage, didn't pay any attention to his house, which was falling apart, and left his mother to waste away in abject poverty.

Meanwhile, Master Augusto Bóia, crushed by the impotence of his frustrated hatreds, grew old, gloomy and dejected, seated in his wicker chair behind the counter in the deserted establishment.

And so the years rolled by—some better, with enough rain, soft winds, abundant corn; others worse, dry, windy, lean harvests.

Francisco Marroco and Maria had another child—a girl whom they named Ludovina.

And Francisco Marroco, reintegrated into the life of the Island—the life he had lived in the lands and on the seas of the World seemed a dream to him—worked the way everybody else did. He went to the shore and out to sea to catch the fish his family ate; he dug, worked the land, turned the land, tied to the handle of his pick and to the beam of the plow; on his back and on the burro's packsaddle he loaded

the wood for the fire and the myrtle and incense branches for the fattening pig's sty. If some friend, his father, Maria, chided him for slaving away so much—"I don't understand why you spent all that time in America and why you've got money earning interest in the bank"—he'd answer without hesitation:
"It's good for a man's health for him to work for his own with what he owns!"
And when at nightfall, all tired out, he came into the house... Everything all tidy! Flowers on the tables and on the shelves; the floor so well scrubbed that it was enough to make a man not want to touch it with his feet and make him want to kiss it; and the fire alight in the hearth in the corner of the kitchen, and Maria and the children, growing up happy, with full tummies, clean and well-clothed bodies. And his mother and his father...

They lived, Francisco Marroco's mother and father, their last days flooded with peace and contentment, with those children who filled the four walls of that house and the hearts of their son and daughter-in-law.
The two old people rocked their grandchildren's cradle. They watched over them while they slept. They felt their fragile bodies in their bony hands. They drank in the innocence of their smiles with their dulled eyes. They heard the babbling of their first sounds with their stiff ears. They supported their first steps with the strength of their frailty. The first stories of fairies and princesses which delighted the hearts of the children—it was they, the grandparents, who told them the stories. And to lull them to sleep, even as they got older, the old man played his guitar and his companion sang softly:

Black goblin—oh...oh...oh...—
Fly away from the roof!
Let the child sleep,
black goblin!—oh...oh...oh...—
a restful little sleep!

He played, she sang. And one day she died. They carried her off in the coffin—and he was beside himself when he felt they were tearing away half of his own body, half of his own being. And he groaned in the pain of his grief:

"You won't have to wait long for me, dear heart!"

As if trying to get away from himself, he threw himself even more into his devotion for the grandchildren. People could still hear him play his guitar—for his grandchildren, only for his grandchildren. They were unknown melodies, childishly simple, which he strummed slowly with his trembling, hesitating fingers. Soothing melodies like the sad winter evenings, the fall of the rain on Autumn mornings, the lament of the waves on nights with a full moon. That is how the old man played—when, at the end of the sea, the sun wasted away in the stillness and silence of the calm afternoon, which transfigured the silhouette of the mountains, the shadow of the trees, the coloring of the flowers, wings and clouds which hovered in the sky, waters of the ocean and cliffs of the coast.

One afternoon—it was in the Spring—two tears fell from his eyes. Longings. He might have been remembering, by chance, his gentle companion. And the tears kept falling from his eyes, which were fixed on the children, who were also transfigured by the stillness and silence of the twilight.

Tired. He felt so tired! And that longing—so strong it would not fit in his heart—the longing for his beloved companion...

And he asked the Lord to take him to her.

He died when the music being played for Pentecost Sunday was heard outside the door. There were those who said they had seen a smile on his lips as he was being lowered into his grave, just as if he were a happy suitor on his way to meet the girl of his dreams.

Francisco Marroco kept that smile of his father's in his heart. He too would die smiling—happy to leave his children in the World with a nice and peaceful life.

It was his great hope.

(but the wheel of fate began to run off the road)

By the time the First World War was over, the situation of the whaling company had gotten so serious that it became almost impossible to keep going. Shareholders and whalers, wherever they were, joined in a hue and cry against the directors—mainly against Augusto Bóia: "A bum!"

Idalina's Joaquim, in his establishment, which was the main place for meetings, pretended he was trying to calm people down:

"Come on, now! Master Augusto is an honorable man! And if you want to see for yourselves whether he is or not, bring up everything you have to discuss when there's a meeting to settle accounts."

There weren't any more meetings to settle accounts, except for once a year, and that one was also the only annual convocation, in general assembly, of the shareholders and whalers of the operation.

"Well, bring all those things up. Examine or have someone you trust examine the books and records."

"Could you do it?"

"Could I!? No, no. Anybody else. And you should elect new directors, if you don't want the ones you've got."

It wouldn't be easy. All of them on one side perhaps

wouldn't be enough to go against the capital subscribed by the old directors. They would have to convince the women's group to support them and, above all, to count on Francisco Marroco—with the weight of his shares. And they got themselves organized and went knocking on door after door.

Bóia wept when he found out about the move. They had stolen his customers—they were trying to oust him from among the whaling company's directors, without realizing that only he, with his experience, could save it. That is what he sincerely and bitterly thought. And, taking heart:

"Backstabbing by the *americano* and that bastard Joaquim! They think I'm finished, but they're wrong!" he said with rage and hatred. And with his allies, he, too, canvassed the village:

"If we can hang on to half a dozen small shareholders, they won't tear our place on the board away from us."

It was a night in January with gale-force winds, and the boatshed was packed. For the first time, the women showed up. Whalers, who, besides being there to receive their pittance, were granted, by tradition, the right to speak came also. And Idalina's Joaquim was there.

Master Augusto Bóia entered with his lackeys on the board behind him. He was lugging the papers and the account book, which he tossed on top of the bottom of an upside-down wooden tub, on which the flame of a tallow candle burned uncertainly . The three sat down around the tub, and Master Augusto spoke with apparent sincerity:

"Once again, as is the custom, I shall read the accounts."

"This year, it'll be slower," they groused. "We want to see the accounts!" And they called out, "Hey, Joaquim!"

"But, thi... this m...man is not a whaler, nor a shareholder!" protested Bóia.

"He's here on our orders!" And those voices tolerated no resistance.

Meanwhile, Francisco Marroco looked at those walls, that nautical equipment stored there, those boats. He had attended another settling of accounts many years earlier when Bóia still fawned all over him. It had been enough for him to see that in a meeting like that, there was nothing to discuss, that everything had been discussed and settled in advance. There weren't even dividends to receive, and only lamentations to be heard. Now, however, since they had asked him, he had not refused to be present. And without knowing how, he began to speak, with emotion. He evoked the person of Captain Silvestre and his generous intention, which perhaps only he, Francisco Marroco, understood because of what he had learned in the World. He predicted the sad end of the company if they continued to stray from the way outlined initially. He proposed that they again raise whalers to the category of partners—and to do that, as the captain had done in another time, they could, given their limited resources, transfer shares in exchange for small withholdings from the pay the whalers would receive. This—even with the risk involved, even with the possible resignation of partners who didn't go out whaling and had no relatives or heirs who might. That's how it ought to be—for the good of the land and so that those who worked could retake control over their work and fight for the survival of the company. The first order of business, however, was the issue of the immediate and total renovation of the flotilla: the construction of boats and a good launch so they could compete with rival boats and raise funds in the short run.

The bystanders laughed to themselves at Francisco Marroco's suggestions. They would have accepted the last one, which meant nothing new, if he had shown he might loosen his purse strings. But Francisco Marroco offered only to be a co-signer at the Bank. And, disillusioned, he heard the arguments raised against him: a launch was just an unnecessary luxury. Their fathers and grandfathers had always gotten whales without having to smell the stink of gasoline. The boats were worn-out, but still usable. The bad of it was... They should let Joaquim finish.

Inside himself, Joaquim was beaming. He had proved nothing against Master Augusto Bóia. In reality what he was interested in was to discredit the one who had been the man of greatest prestige in the village and one of the ones who had picked on him when he was a child. The others would lose nothing in the delay. And he lifted his head and his words came out dull, slow, well-worn:

"It would be better to call on someone else. The schoolmaster, the priest, for example."

"Here we don't want anyone else! Spit it out!"

"I've always had the greatest respect for Master Augusto."

"What we want to know is what it says in all those papers! And right now!"

"It seems to me there's a mistake. Three *contos* unaccounted for..."

"That's a lie!" shouted Bóia. "Stinking liar! Stinking liar!!!"

They didn't hear him. They hadn't heard him for a long time. They would never hear him again.

"Thief! Throw him out! Thief!" roared men, screeched women. An angry hand brutally grabbed Bóia's body and threw it, like a useless burden, out the door with the directors' lackeys behind him.

And in that climate of exaltation, those moneyless accounts were closed and elections were held.

There was no one among the new directors who understood accounts. That is why they gave Idalina's Joaquim the responsibility for the books and, so there would be no slip-ups, they granted him full power of attorney. And then they relaxed, they all relaxed, except Francisco Marroco.

Travel by sailing ship had died out a long time before. The Crowns had left Faial, and the new buyer of whale oil was Mister Chico Gaudêncio.

Mister Chico Gaudêncio had been born poor on the Rua Velha. He had grown up with the bay area roughnecks, within the sight of sailors coming off foreign ships anchored there, who wanted a guide to take them to the houses of prostitution. The last Crown had taken a liking to him. He gave him a job and they left him the master of everything on the Island which had belonged to the family.

Other buyers of whale oil set up businesses on Faial and Pico. Nevertheless, those responsible for the old operations, those attached to the usual establishment, transferred to the new businessman the esteem they felt for the former businessmen. And they didn't regret it. Where the Americans set no time limit on credit used to buy materials for boat repairs, Mister Chico Gaudêncio also didn't mind waiting. The only thing was that while the Americans paid for the oil promptly, Chico Gaudêncio, even though he waited for what he was owed, made people wait much longer for what he owed them. They didn't hold it against him because business wasn't so good.

In spite of everything, Mister Chico Gaudêncio moved on to bigger things. He set up his own operation. He had bought the company at Porto Pim. He placed around Faial newly constructed boats and launches equipped with motors so powerful that other ones couldn't point their prows at them. It was said he intended to expand to Pico and it was feared he would do so.

Everywhere there was talk of Mister Chico Gaudêncio

and his business activities. Where would the man have gotten the money to do so much in such a short time? It was quietly hinted that it was probably from the Our Lady of Life Bank.

The new directors of the local whaling company received a strange letter from Mister Chico Gaudêncio. It informed them of an overdue debt and requested the presence of a responsible person in his office on Faial for the purpose of agreeing on a way to settle the matter.

Idalina's Joaquim went with the power of attorney in his pocket. On his return, he called the directors and locked himself up with them in his shop. The debt in question had been increasing for about four years, and Mister Chico Gaudêncio, informed of the latest developments, demanded, uncharacteristically, its liquidation in six months.

They convoked an extraordinary general assembly. The few shareholders who responded to the call renewed their allegations against Bóia and concluded that even selling the boats, damaged as they were, wouldn't raise enough to pay off half the amount. But the directors should decide. And the directors—Joaquim should decide because that's what they paid him for.

Time passed and nothing was decided. Some small amount of thought was given to a loan. There was even talk of approaching Francisco Marroco. They knocked at his door. The six months would be over in three days.

Francisco Marroco had become disillusioned with the whaling company. And he had his life to lead, his family. His children were in school, António in the second grade, Ludovina in the first. It was lovely to see them at night, at home, seated around the table, with Maria next to them, teaching them their lessons. And in the morning, gathered together with their companions, they ran off to school with their book-bags over their shoulders. Francisco Marroco set off for his fields—and worked like a slave!

He didn't touch his money, which was in the Bank, waiting for his children. His children in school, his children in the *liceu*, his children in Coimbra... The dream which would become a reality.

And Joaquim went to Faial without a penny in his pocket. He promised, hesitatingly, to get an extension, the granting of an amortization, sometime in the future, on the oil they'd sell.

Mister Chico Gaudêncio, comfortably seated at his desk, was not interested in the oil from possible future whales still swimming freely in the sea: either they met the set conditions, which were generous they would have to admit, or he would foreclose.

Standing before him, Joaquim understood: he was right, no one could deny it, Mister Chico Gaudêncio had waited quite a bit! But...

"Four years! Almost five!" Mister Chico Gaudêncio was impressed with his own complacency. "I can't wait any longer! I can't! If it were anyone else, it would have been... a long time ago."

He was right, really quite right! Joaquim nodded in agreement. A court case, now, would mean a lot of trouble.

Trouble Mister Chico Gaudêncio wanted to avoid! But he had to settle that matter. Unless... And suddenly, he was very cordial:

"Mr. Joaquim is the person who can."

"Me?!"

"Yes, yes! Don't you have the power of attorney?!"

"Yes, sir, I do, but..."

"Well, if you were willing..."

And Mister Chico Gaudêncio spoke quietly in a deep voice: "It would lose money, no doubt about it. At any rate... The old operation could not last. And instead of an outsider taking it over..." If Mr. Joaquim were willing, he would make him the manager. He lived far away and he needed a person he could trust. And only then did he discreetly point to a chair: "But, sit down, sit down!"

"Thank you! Thank you very much!"

Really, he wasn't cut out to be a manager. Mister Chico Gaudêncio could easily find someone better for the job.

"No, sir! I won't find anybody. All we have to do is to stop by the notary."

"It's the law that..."

"The law's what I want it to be! The notary works for me."

The matter was settled. Mister Chico Gaudêncio, under the pretext of paying himself what they owed him, took over the village's company.

A powerful launch, which carried on board Idalina's Joaquim, the representative of the new owner, towed in the boats to replace those Captain Silvestre had brought from America, along with his ideal of a whaling cooperative.

Everyone saw. And Francisco Marroco thought sadly:

"They used to be free men, the whalers of my country. Today, they have become slaves like all slaves of the World." He felt no remorse for having refused the loan. "The problem is not just the lack of money!"

And Mister Chico Gaudêncio brought in more boats: on Pico, on the north side, at Cais; on São Jorge, in the town of Velas; on Graciosa, at Santa Cruz.

Such prosperity was astounding. The price for building and outfitting a boat was up beyond reach, the motor for a launch cost a fortune, to tell the truth—and Mister Chico Gaudêncio sent to sea boats and motor launches bought in England and in Germany like a smoker spitting the pieces of a cigarette butt onto the ground. If he were to move more slowly... The way he was going, no matter how well things went...

It was held, openly, that everything was owed to favors from the Our Lady of Life Bank. It was loudly proclaimed that whoever was running it was going the wrong way—and taking poor care of monies belonging to others.

All those who hadn't gotten together the hoped-for deposit consoled themselves by circulating and adding to the rumors. The others got alarmed. And they got more alarmed when it spread that Chico Gaudêncio had let the deadline go by and hadn't paid on a note come due at the Our Lady of Life Bank. It was added that he refused to honor his obligations and that the total amount attributed to them was so great that by carrying his debts forward there was reason to fear for the solvency of the Bank.

Francisco Marroco went to Faial. He expressed his fears (through "people are saying that...") to the director, who received him courteously as always and explained to him: the Our Lady of Life Bank had extended credit to Mister Chico Gaudêncio, with security, of course, because it believed his activities to be a contribution to the development of the region. It had had no regrets until a short while before, since Mister Chico Gaudêncio had never failed to meet his obligations. Only now... But Mister Francisco Marroco should have no doubts: Mister Chico Gaudêncio would pay—oh, he would pay!—one way or another.

"So you think my money's running no risk?"

"None at all! We're in June. Holidays begin in August. By October everything will be settled."

"I'm very grateful to you!" And Francisco Marroco came away not knowing that if he had insisted on withdrawing his money, the Bank would not have been able to give it to him.

(and misfortune came in that year of drought and of cyclone)

It had rained for the last time in the beginning of May. In the middle of July, the corn was lost in the dry fields, and not a drop of water remained in the cisterns and empty tanks.

The farmers sent their livestock to the woods and kept only burros, horses and mules which might be useful in the struggle against the scourge of the drought close to their doors.

Throughout the whole day—from Calheta, from Fetais, from Jogo da Bola, from Feteira, from Ribeira Grande, from Piedade, from Cruz do Redondo, from Caminho Largo, from Alta-Mora, from Ponta da Ilha, from Calhau, from Ribeirinha—the crowds walked up and down, cans, water jugs, clothing tubs on the heads of the women, on the shoulders of the men and on the backs of the animals. And Francisco Marroco and Maria went, too, like everyone else, at the crack of dawn, in the midst of the multitude, the two of them walking behind their little burro. They were long journeys, more than two hours each way.

The water in the swamp had become mud—and from the mud, people squeezed the drop which quenched their thirst and washed their clothes. Mud, too, was what the water of the pools and the ponds in the uplands and in the pastures had become—and the livestock was dying of hunger and thirst because there was no longer anything but earth to eat and mud to drink.

And the wandering began. People recalled fearfully what the old ones said about the other years of drought. Francisco Marroco remembered what he'd heard from his Grandmother.

They burned laurel in the belief that the smoke from the laurel would keep them safe from harm, but no one drank the water from the swamp without first boiling it.

Idalina's Joaquim went from house to house, fully carrying out his duties as someone who *understood things*. He peeked at whitened tongues, he took pulses, prescribed pills and enemas. The wretched ones lived with their souls hanging from his gestures and words. Sometimes he advised them to go to the physician, who lived far away, in the town, a distance of five leagues, and didn't dare set out on those horrible roads, not even for the equivalent of two pay envelopes from whaling. And one pay envelope, just one, was as much as entered most of the homes in the course of a year.

The church bells tolled the first signs of death, of the desolation of the fields and of the hearts of the people.

Francisco Marroco went to the burials of those who fell—and he, Maria, and all of them continued dragging themselves through the sorrowful calvary of drought—emaciated, feet no longer able to bear the sharp edges of the stones on the road, legs no longer able to stand from the time spent on the day's walking, eyes shaded from the sky which was awash with sun and wiped clean of clouds, their mouths wide open, swallowing even the last dregs from that bitter chalice.

And Maria—Maria, too!—fell to bed. Joaquim prescribed. Her fever went up. Thirty-eight; thirty-nine point six, seven, eight, nine... And Maria, white as the lime on the walls, stretched out there on the bed.

Masses of black clouds grew in the southeast and rolled across the sky—for the first time in four months. They took them to be the harbingers of rain—and all they did was vomit out cyclone-force winds!

The walls and the roofs of the houses trembled. Leaves from cornstalks, from grapevines, from fig trees, from myrtles, from the incense trees whirled around. The sea became rough, thundering in enormous waves against the rocky coast. Peoples withdrew, sadder in spirit and more crestfallen under the weight of that additional misfortune.

In Francisco Marroco's home, late in the afternoon, Maria was delirious. She did not understand what people said to her, her breathing was labored, her pulse pounding and rapid. The thermometer showed more than forty degrees, and Joaquim didn't know what to do:

"The doctor! It's better to call the doctor!" And Francisco Marroco looked at Joaquim, his eyes wide open: "No, no!" Maria was sick, very sick. But the doctor... And he held Joaquim in an iron grip:

"The doctor!? We have to call the doctor!? We have to!? We have to!?

His children looked at him—and he felt their eyes begging him for a decision from his authority and wisdom as a father.

The doctor wouldn't come at night for any amount of money—and he'd be even less likely to do so in that weather. And Maria ...No! He had to go! He had to save Maria!

A door. A straw mattress. On it—Maria, delirious, babbling words no one could understand, waving her hands about uncontrollably. Maria—mute, blind, unconscious. Maria—smothering in piles of clothing which were secured against the wind by interlaced twine. Maria—laid out on the straw mattress, which eight men carried in shifts, four at a time!

They left the house in the dead of night. And their children sobbing in the doorway. And the compassionate presence of their neighbors. And the omen of the old women with black shawls over their heads!

And the black sky, and the sea roaring against the shore, and leaves from myrtles, from the incense trees, from cornstalks, from the vines, carried off by the air and whistling in the darkness of the night like lost souls!

And the men, shaken by the claws of the wind, lashed on by the whip of agony on that long journey of more than five hours—moving on, moving on, moving on, quickly, quickly! Constantly moving and always quickly, quickly, souls tormented, bodies clammy with sweat, legs shaky from weariness, stumbling on stones, stumbling in holes!... And they...—still going on and always quickly, quickly climbing and going down stony outcroppings bad enough to make a horse stumble, wrapped in the swirling wind and in the blackness of the gloomy night!...

At two in the morning, they set the mattress down on the ground at the doctor's door. Under the blankets, Maria—as if on fire, delirious, hands limp from fatigue, lips still murmuring imperceptibly.

Francisco Marroco knocked—fearfully, because the physician didn't like his sleep to be disturbed. He knocked again—more forcefully, more forcefully, and more quickly, more quickly.

The doctor stuck his head out angrily:

"This isn't the garden door! Office hours start at nine in the morning!" And he slammed the window in Francisco Marroco's face with all its desperation and pain.

Greater than the fury of the wind and sea, the storm in the hearts of those men exploded deafeningly. They broke down the door, raced up the stairs, went down halls, went through bedrooms, looked, looked again and grabbed the doctor in his underwear, hiding, terrified, behind the hearthstone in the kitchen.

Back outside, next to Maria, Francisco Marroco held in his hands the hands of his love—those calloused, chapped, work-stained hands. Those hands... in the gloomy night.

(And there was the other distant night when the grapes were being picked... His father playing his guitar, his mother by his side; the couples whirling around in the turns of the *chamarrita*; and the night filled with stars and moonlight... He and she were two children. And those hands were fine,

spoiled, delicate. After, the return from America, the wedding night...)
The wind kicked against the walls of the gardens and the sides of the houses. On the shore, the tide was cursing.
By the time the men reappeared, kicking the doctor along in front of them, Francisco Marroco already felt the stillness and the cold of death in those beloved hands he kept holding in his.

And everything fell apart and was lost for Francisco Marroco: happiness, fortune, the dream and the life he'd dreamt of for his children.
Mister Chico Gaudêncio did not pay the Our Lady of Life Bank what he owed. He got divorced, remarried, with separate property, the woman from whom he'd gotten divorced, and showed up in court with no assets of his own. Because of that embezzlement—and others which the trial brought shockingly to light—the Our Lady of Life Bank failed. And those who'd entrusted their savings to it were left with nothing.
And the drought and the winds had swept away whatever man had sown on the lands of the Island.
At that moment, however, everything meant nothing to Francisco Marroco! A human ragbag, tatters of despair, he spent the days shut up in his room, on the bed, without sleeping, without speaking, without eating, motionless, his eyes fixed on the ceiling. In that room, on that bed—he felt Maria's presence.
Nor did he get up when he heard about the steamship which arrived with the corn the generous Azoreans laboring in America sent in an act of solidarity so that the Year of the Famine wouldn't be repeated.
And it was the children—António was no older than nine—who asked the man in charge of distribution for a bag

of corn. They asked him with the voices of children who had not been raised to ask for things. They asked him for it with the tears of motherless children.

The first time he went out—for the sake of his children he had to keep on living and struggling—Francisco Marroco ran into Master Augusto Bóia, who was dragging his unsteady legs and leaning on a cane.

And Master Augusto Bóia stopped in front of him, looked at him dressed like that in deep mourning —he looked at him with his resentful eyes—and he said:

"Well, if it isn't the *americano*..."

And he laughed. The old man laughed with his toothless mouth diabolically, scornfully.

That was the last time anyone called Francisco the *americano*.

PART THREE

AND THAT NIGHT THERE WERE NO STARS IN THE SKY

That night, when António Marroco entered the store, which was poorly lit by the lamp hanging from a beam, Mister Joaquim was already getting up, putting on his glasses, and opening the old banged-up book of the whaling accounts, which was on the pine table in front of him. Because of the war which had broken out—the Second World War—oil brought prices never dreamed of before. On Faial, in the port of Comprido, and on Pico, in São Mateus, the whalers were getting pay envelopes of twenty, twenty-five and thirty contos.

The pay envelopes of the whalers in the village never had more than three contos—and were always distributed after excessively long delays. On land and at sea, free from eavesdropping ears and prying eyes, they vented the full fury of their bitterness against Mister Chico Gaudêncio and Mister Joaquim: "The bastards, they're stolen what we've earned by our work!" And they added under their breaths: "They're such a bunch of bastards they're not ashamed to do business with the German submarines."

There, however, they looked, murky eyes hiding behind the smoke of their cigarettes, at Mister Chico Gaudêncio, white-haired, wearing his expensive suit and smoking his fine-smelling cigar, sitting on an empty line spool, and heard Mister Joaquim, who read in a slow nasal voice:

"Accounts of the 'Union and Brotherhood Whaling Operation' for the year... (Two and a half years had passed since the last one): "On such and such a date: *so many* whales harpooned; oil yielded: *so many* tons; gross receipts: *so much*: expenses: *so much;* net receipts: *so much*...

An excessively long and tiresome reading; António, meanwhile, was doing his figuring in his head. Mister Joaquim, on cue from Mister Gaudêncio, mentioned at the right moment that oil was selling for *so much* a kilo. It seemed strange to him not to hear repeated, as was customary on accounts day, that *"so much* a kilo"... Well, so many tons at so much a kilo...

But Mister Joaquim was getting to the end:

"Total receipts: *so much;* total expenses (fuel and lubricants for the launch motors, repairs to the boats, purchase of equipment, payment of the lookouts and of himself, Joaquim, in his capacity as manager): *so much;* 50% of the net receipts to the owner: *so much;* 50% of the net receipts for the whalers: *so much;* it comes down to fifty-one pay envelopes with two thousand four hundred and two escudos and five centavos per envelope.

Mister Joaquim put the ledger down on the pine table and took off his glasses:

"The accounts have been read. Does everyone accept them?" And his tired and inexpressive eyes scanned the hard, impenetrable faces of the whalers.

Reviving what he had learned at school, António kept on with his mental arithmetic: *"So many* tons of oil are... Three places to the right, three places to the right gives *so many* kilos. At *so much* a kilo... *This* times *that*, and two, and three..." And then, taken aback: *so many* tons at *so much* a kilo equalled *so much*! His figures did not agree with Mister

Joaquim's figures! He took a nervous drag on his cigarette. He looked at his companions. He sensed in them the same uneasiness, the same suspicion, the same accusation. As well as the same fear of Mister Chico Gaudêncio. But mostly of Mister Joaquim.

No whaler, not even the best of the officers, dared stand up to Mister Joaquim. Mister Chico Gaudêncio was the proprietor, the boss. But he lived far away. It was Mister Joaquim who was always there, dealing with the whalers. Now that Master Augusto Bóia had been dead for a long time, he owned the only establishment in those parts. He sold on credit to the whalers. When there was little corn during the years of drought and winds, he loaned the escudos needed to buy bread. And he waited for the money he loaned and for the twenty percent interest until they divided the whaling money, which had to pass through his manager's hands. It was also he, only he, who, when sickness came, appeared in the whalers' homes with the hope of cure. It would be bold indeed for anyone to challenge the murky waters of the ill will of Mister Joaquim, who spoke again, commandingly:

"Since no one had anything to say, let the officers come forward to sign the accounts."

Six of the oldest men tossed the butts of their cigarettes on the ground, crushing them under their pigskin sandals, and moved up to the pine table.

"Come, come!" And Mister Joaquim put his glasses back on and read the ritual phrase: *"We declare the accounts in order and we consider ourselves paid and satisfied."*

"What a load of shit!" murmured António without being heard. And he took a deeper drag. The others also took deeper drags on their cigarettes.

Mister Joaquim pushed the ledger to the edge of the table, dipped the stick-pen into the ordinary ink of the inkwell and handed it to the officer in front:

"Here. Sign here, on this line!"

"??"

"Yes, yes! On this line!"

Bent over, with great effort, the man tried to scratch down his name with his heavy, clumsy hand.

The crewmen, oppressed and undecided, looked at him. The officers spoke for all of them. If with their signatures they endorsed those accounts, they would all lose the right to ask for explanations, to protest, to cry out for justice. But the fear...

Unexpectedly, however, a voice broke down the silence:

"The master will not sign, because we want to ask some questions."

The officer paused with the stick-pen in the air. Joaquim took his glasses away from his shadowy eyes. Mister Chico Gaudêncio tried to light the cigar which he held in his mouth, already lit.

The whalers turned toward the one who had had the unheard-of courage to speak—old João Laró, older than the oldest of the officers, loaded with children, even grandchildren, still standing straight and tall, head held proudly high. A sailor of the first order, he had never made it to the rank of officer, which was very much desired because it meant a share twice what a crew member got, nor to harpooner, which meant one and a half times what the others got—only because he had unbendingly refused to give up his neck to the yoke of servitude, and become tame and submissive as a castrated ox.

"And what do you want to know?" inquired Mister Chico Gaudêncio condescendingly.

"Wasn't the oil sold for *so much* a kilo?"

"You don't want to know about anything else?"

"No. Nothing else."

"In reality, that's the price quoted. But..."

"Then there's been a mistake. By my figures, we should be getting at least five hundred escudos more per pay envelope."

"You're right. We were getting to that point."

"You were getting to that point... That you were, but you didn't."

"In fact," and Mister Chico Gaudêncio did let on he understood the insinuation, "we settled on a price, as you note. Then the price dropped and we lost five centavos a kilo. That's what happened."

"You lost! And those on Faial and at Cais made out. Good! It doesn't seem to me that we have anything to do with that loss. You received the oil at *so much,* and it's at that amount you have to pay us our share!"

"Man! I already explained it!"

"Yes, and very nicely explained. Still, what I'd like to hear you tell us is that if instead of losing you'd made five centavos more a kilo than you'd expected, you'd pass on to us the difference above that you'd promised us."

"That'll be the day!" grumbled the whalers, all fear gone now, fortified by such daring.

Mister Chico Gaudêncio couldn't find the words:

"Well... I, you..."

"No more of this!" Mister Joaquim was getting angry.

"Shut your trap, you worthless quack! We've known each other for a long time!" And João Laró, without batting an eyelash: "What we ought to do is not accept those accounts. If everybody agrees with me..."

"We're with you!" shouted the whalers all together.

"Let's demand our rights! Let's go to the Port Authority!"

"Let's go! Let's go!"

And they left—except for the six officers and two harpooners—they all left in a mob, roaring like a wave about to crest, swollen with fury:

"Thieves! They're worse than the whores they had for mothers! Thieves!"

That had never happened before. It had better not ever happen. With a sinister look of understanding—a terribly sinister look—Mister Chico Gaudêncio and Mister Joaquim glanced at each other.

"My launch is at the pier ready to go," said the former.

"You people sign the accounts," ordered the latter. And, noting that the officers hesitated: "Go on, on with it, the boss is in a hurry!"

"Six contos extra for each one," suggested Mister Chico Gaudêncio, persuasively.

"Quickly now!" insisted Joaquim. "There's no time to lose! We have to get to the town before that rabble!"

And they boarded the launch Mister Chico Gaudêncio had waiting for him at the pier.

Mister Chico Gaudêncio and Mister Joaquim simply went to have a few words with the Port Captain. As proof of what they were saying, they showed him the accounts properly signed by the officers, who accompanied them, and witnessed by the two harpooners, who also went with them. All honest people.

When the whalers reached the Port Authority's doors, they were met by the coastguardsmen and the shore patrol, from the section commanded by the sergeant, both armed with rifles. And they were all arrested.

Francisco Marroco dragged himself to the town to see the whalers and his son—his son!—behind bars. With him, in tears, went his daughter-in-law and daughter, still unmarried, and his terrified grandchildren.

He felt himself suddenly old, very, very old.

He returned home defeated forever.

It was night.

And on that night, as on so many others, there were no stars in the sky.